Resort to Love

Resort to Love

A Paradise Key Romance

Priscilla Oliveras

TULE
PUBLISHING

Dedication

As always, to *mi familia*—Mami, Papi, and my girls…without you my life would lack color and joy and have far less love. *¡Los quiero mucho!*

Sincere *gracias* going out to

Jackie, *hermana* extraordinaire, for the brainstorming & beta reading that helped bring Sofía and Nate's story to life.

JD, the beautiful writing desk you crafted for me created the perfect spot for inspiration; I love you, little brother!

Tom, for answering all my questions & attempting to give me a crash course in basic property acquisition when my deadline loomed.

Any mistakes are all mine!

Susan, Kyra, and Shirley, for the camaraderie & kinship throughout my first continuity experience.

Alexis, Mia & Sabrina, for the pep talks when doubts loomed; it's such an incredible blessing to have you as part of my writing *familia*!
#4ChicasChat #LatinxRom

For my fellow Latinx romance authors and all romance Authors of Color, may our stories be told and celebrated—*¡Siempre!*

Chapter One

*F*UN AND GAMES. *No strings attached.*

That had been her and Nate's mentality all those years ago. Faulty though it might have been.

Heart weighed down by sadness, Sofía Vargas stared across the street at the peeling paint and storm-damaged sign indicating Paradise Key Resort, once a significant part of her home away from home. She gripped her JavaStop paper coffee cup as memories sluiced over her like one of the daily summer rain showers they dealt with along this part of the Florida Gulf Coast.

Ay, the folly of youth and immaturity.

One thing life had taught her so far was that the fun and games eventually came to an abrupt halt. Oftentimes without any notice or warning.

Out of habit, she made a quick sign of the cross, pressing a kiss to her fingertips at the end and offering up a prayer for sweet Lily. Gone far too soon, leaving a gaping hole in their Fabulous Five-some.

Dios mío, none of the girls had ever thought they'd reunite in their old stomping grounds for one of their own funerals. Not this soon in life anyway.

Tears threatening again, Sofía sucked in a breath and stepped into the road to cross 2nd Street, unable to resist the resort's pull.

No strings attached.

Those words haunted her. Or more like mocked her.

She had tossed them out without thinking when she and Nate had hooked up the summer before their junior year of high school. Years later, she realized it had been a defense mechanism on her part. Though a flawed one. Because despite her claim to the contrary and the miles that had separated them over the years, she'd never quite been able to cut all the threads that bound her to him.

Not that she'd admit it to anyone. Not even the girls.

A chica had to keep a secret or two buried. Locked away until they shriveled up and died. Hopefully.

Staring at the pale peach stucco facade of the resort's main building, its grand arched entrance that had once invitingly beckoned the rich and on-the-cusp-of famous guests, now looking forlorn and lost, Sofía felt herself falling back into the bittersweet memories of her adolescence.

Oh, the naivety of first love. The pain of her first heartbreak, made worse by the swift kick of harsh reality.

Those two fun-filled, intense summers with Nate, the dalliances they'd shared in the years after…they all came crashing down on her as if the calm waters of the Gulf of Mexico had suddenly risen in a tidal wave of love, loss, and immature expectations.

The dilapidated resort had once been a symbol of deep ties and hopeful possibilities. Coming to Paradise Key each summer to stay with Tía Milagros was how Sofía had met her closest friends. Back then, they'd been the power of five. Today, because of Lily's car accident, they were down to a forlorn four.

Sofía's chest ached with the bitter loss that bound her, Evie, Lauren, and Jenna. A bond none of the girls wanted.

Getting the call about Lily's death last week had knocked Sofía to her knees. Just days earlier, the two of them had spoken about Sofía coming up from Key West as soon as business slowed down. Why had she waited so long to visit Paradise Key?

Bueno, she knew why.

To avoid reminders of Nate.

Learning about Lily's accident had been a horrific, life-changing moment. One that had dragged Sofía back to this sleepy beachside town that had been both her refuge and the catalyst for the fire that fueled her professional drive. Especially when others had expected, even predicted, her failure.

She stepped onto the cracked sidewalk, her eyes lingering on the blue and white *for-sale* sign hammered into the ground in the barren flowerbed. The large block lettering announced the date and time for the combined Historic Review Board and Local Planning Agency meeting interested parties should attend.

As luck would have it, the meeting was next week. If it

could be considered lucky that she was in town for one of her best friend's funeral.

A humid spring breeze blew Sofía's hair into her face, and she tossed the dark tresses back. She squinted into the late afternoon sun, turning her gaze away from the resort to stare at the wooden pier extending into the Gulf waters off to the right. Tourists and locals strolled along the walkway, some stopping to take in the view. Others paused to sit on one of the wooden benches dotting the length of the pier, enjoying the crisp spring weather. Overhead, a flock of seagulls squawked their arrival. They glided through the air, crisscrossing and taking turns dive-bombing into the ocean for fish.

The familiar smells of sun, sand, and lazy surf brought a bittersweet smile to her lips as she thought of happier times. When she, Lily, Evie, Lauren, and Jenna had whiled away the hours sprawled on towels in the sand, tanning oil slathered on their skin. *Bueno*, except for Jenna. With her auburn hair and light skin tone, Jenna had spent more time under a beach umbrella complaining about the unfairness of DNA and envying Sofía's Latina tan.

Ay, the fun their group had cooked up over the summers when they could all be together. Sofía had loved coming up from Miami to stay with her *tía* while her two younger brothers headed to Puerto Rico to spend time with their abuela. Evie and Lauren traveled down to stay at Paradise Key Resort with their families. Jenna and Lily, lucky girls, lived on Paradise Key year-round.

From the age of pigtails through high school graduation, Sofía lived for those summers with the people she'd come to think of as her Paradise Key *familia,* by blood or by choice. One-on-one time with her *tía.* Frolicking with her best girlfriends. And, near the end, during those last two summers, Nate had shown up on the scene, ordered by his father to "learn the ropes" of the family business by working in the resort office, one of Hamilton's smaller properties. Their forbidden romance—him in management, her a summer employee—had heightened their adolescent hormones. Until...

Shaking off the hurtful memories, Sofía turned back to the *for-sale* sign.

Dios mío, could she pull this off? Was she crazy enough to think she could get the financial backing to actually buy this place?

While she'd been busy clawing her way up the hospitality and hotel management food chain, currently overseeing several B&Bs in Key West, the resort had been left abandoned and forlorn. Storm-damaged, barely a shadow of its once-flourishing grandeur.

This place had been her entrance into her chosen field. Working beside her *tía* in housekeeping, and then later moving on to a lifeguard position and shifts as waitstaff in the pool area, had given her a taste of the industry. It was what led her to major in Hospitality Administration in college. And it'd been old man Hamilton's condescending attitude during their one private conversation that had prepared her for the roadblocks she would face throughout her career.

Maybe old man Hamilton had been right—maybe she and Nathan didn't belong together—but that hadn't been his decision to make.

She might have only been nineteen, but she'd had a strong enough sense of self to throw old man Hamilton's bribe back in his face. One of her proudest life moments had come when she'd made her last student loan payment a few years ago.

A seagull landed on a corner of the *for-sale* sign. Taunting…maybe encouraging her. Sofía hadn't mentioned the idea to her girlfriends yet. But when she did, she imagined Evie and Lauren, having grown up in the world of the rich and entitled, would tell her to give the old man the finger, probably even join her in doing so. Jenna, always the peacemaker, would caution her to not dwell on the past, to not let it influence her decisions today. Lily, well, hopefully she was looking down on them all, ready to be their guardian angel.

Closing her eyes, Sofía took a deep breath, then slowly released it along with the doubts she refused to let crowd in on her.

If she could pull this off…no, *when* she pulled this off…when she became the new owner of Paradise Key Resort, she'd attain her goal of running her own place rather than someone else's.

As a bonus, winning the bid would be like showing the egotistical former Paradise Key Resort owner Nathan Hamilton, II, his son Nate who had hurt her more than she cared to admit, and all those naysayers who had ever blocked her path that they'd been wrong to bet against her.

Si, definitely wrong.

Reaching across with her left arm, Sofía rubbed her fingers over the poker chip tattoo on the back of her right shoulder. No doubt about it, when it came down to it, she'd bet on herself to win any day.

NATHAN HAMILTON, III, eased his rental car into a parking spot on the corner of 2nd and C Streets, a couple of blocks down from Paradise Key Resort.

Travel weary after the flight from New York to Gainesville, Florida, where he'd picked up the convertible and immediately started the hour-plus drive west, he heaved a disgruntled sigh.

This was the absolute *last* place he wanted to be right now. But when Nathan Patrick Hamilton, II, gave an order, no one, including his namesake, disobeyed.

The days of Nate's youthful indiscretions when he'd jumped through loopholes in his father's edicts, fixated on having fun and stretching the lines of propriety, were long gone. Hell, he'd spent most of his adult life trying to live up to his father's vision of a "real Hamilton man." Towing the line at work. Swallowing his complaints when his recommendations fell on deaf ears or were passed along for his father's latest lackey to pursue. Even going so far as to get engaged to a longtime family friend when neither he nor Melanie had really wanted it. But marriage would have been the "right" merger for their two families.

The fact Melanie had seen reason, breaking off their engagement a couple of months ago, while he'd been floundering with how to stand up to their parents on their behalf, still felt like sandpaper rubbing across Nate's skin.

A little lost, a lot pissed off—at no one and everyone all at once—he'd spent several nights swimming in a pool of whiskey, before quickly realizing that wasn't the solution.

His father, in his infinite wisdom, had given Nate his typical pessimistic pep talk, aka ultimatum—figure out how to close a deal as simple as a marriage or risk a demotion within the company.

Not that Nate needed his father's money; he'd already aged into his grandfather's inheritance and could go off on his own. But why create another rift in the family? One Nate knew would only hurt his mom.

When word had gotten them that Paradise Key Resort, once a small gem in their resort jewel box, was back on the market, his dad had banished him down here on a fact-finding mission.

Now a quick glance at his Tag Heuer told Nate he was about fifteen minutes early for his appointment with Tyson Braddock, city commissioner and chair of the town's Local Planning Agency. They'd arranged to meet at the JavaStop across the street from the resort. Nate planned to pick the guy's brain to find out any inside info that would help Hamilton, Inc's bid.

After checking his side mirror to ensure he wouldn't take out a bike rider, Nate opened the driver's side door and slid from his car. The late spring humidity instantly wrapped him in its moist embrace. Granted, it was a far cry better than the mid-summer cloying bear hug of humidity that had locals and tourists thankful for the ocean breezes.

He clicked the auto lock, then slid the keys in his front jeans pocket as he surveyed the area. A strange sort of comfort wormed its way through his chest.

The more things changed, the more they stayed the same.

The main drag of downtown Paradise Key still welcomed visitors with brightly painted shops and beach-themed displays. On the south side of the street, toward the beach one block over, he could see the corner of 1st Street, then Dock Street with its wooden wharf, where restaurants and the town bar, Scallywags, treated patrons to ocean views and killer sunsets.

If he took the time to stroll over, the white sand would tickle his feet, and the warm water would lap against his ankles while the briny air filled his lungs. If he closed his eyes, he'd probably hear her throaty laughter on the wind. One he'd often heard in his dreams when his defenses were down.

But he wasn't here to meander the beach or give into distracting thoughts about what—*whom*—he'd given up.

Instead, he headed toward the JavaStop.

At the corner of Second and Depot, he checked his phone while waiting for a van to pass the intersection. He glanced up, the breath whooshing out of him when he spotted her.

Coffee cup in hand, Sofía Vargas stood on the sidewalk in front of Paradise Key Resort.

The wind ruffled her long black hair, and she tossed it back with a jerk of her neck. Nate's gut clenched. How many times had he seen that same gesture, paired with a cheeky grin or a sexy smirk, aimed his way?

It'd been two years since they'd been together. Two years since she told him not to contact her again. And yet, he'd know that athletic, curvy-hipped figure anywhere. His fingers itched to touch her again.

Before he realized it, Nate had crossed the street toward her. As he stepped onto the sidewalk, she spun around to leave, inadvertently running smack into him.

"Oomph," she grunted. The lid on her coffee popped off, the contents of her cup splashing dangerously close to the rim. "*Ay Dios mío*, I'm so sor—"

She broke off on a gasp, her shock at seeing him telegraphed in her wide hazel eyes.

"Hello, Sofía. It's good to see you again."

Huge understatement.

Her sleeveless light purple sundress hit her mid-thigh, leaving her tanned shoulders and shapely legs bare. Just like he remembered, she looked sun-kissed and amazingly beautiful. Definitely a welcome sight for his sore, bloodshot eyes.

"What are you doing here?" she asked, never one to beat around the bush.

He, despite the surprise of running into her, knew better than to reveal his cards when it came to business. Especially to an ex-lover with close ties to this town. Until he'd gleaned all the info he could from Braddock, and learned whether there were other players in the mix for the resort, he was simply passing through.

"Road tripping," he answered. "Thought I'd swing by Paradise Key, take in the sights."

Sofía's narrow-eyed glare told him he'd laid the schmooze on a little too thick. He'd never been able to easily pull a fast one on her.

"Fine. You caught me. There's a property in Sarasota the family's interested in." True enough. If this deal fell through, he'd be headed south to the other beach town. "I had a few days to kill, so I figured what the hell."

He lifted a shoulder, letting it fall with a lazy shrug.

Sofía mimicked his gesture. "Sure, what the hell. For old time's sake, right?"

Whether she intended to or not, her jab hit him like a cheap shot in the gut.

For old time's sake.

That had been his line. One he'd used over the years whenever he'd given into the urge to see her again, and had shown up on her doorstep. Or convinced her to meet him somewhere for a weekend getaway.

Until he'd told her about his father's demand he put a ring on Melanie's finger—a smart business move for both their families. Until Sofía hadn't asked him *not* to do it.

That's when he'd finally understood that her "no-strings-attached" edict wasn't merely something she flippantly tossed around. She meant it. The part of herself he'd felt she held back from him for some reason would always be a roadblock between them.

His gaze slid past her shoulder to take in Paradise Key Resort, the once-flourishing property now worn and dilapidated. Tired-looking.

Kind of how he felt lately. Questioning the decisions he'd made in trying to please his father. Keeping the peace like his mom in her delicate nature preferred.

The businessman inside him recognized the property's state of disrepair as good news. It would drive the price lower. Make his offer to take the blighted property off the city's hands to bring it back to its old glory an even sweeter deal for the city commissioners. It'd be a bid they couldn't refuse.

He needed this to go smoothly if he wanted his dad off his back.

More importantly, it would help him get his head back in the game.

"She's not the same, is she?" he said.

Sofía's brow creased in a moment of confusion before she angled her body to look back at the resort. "No, it's kind of sad. Though inevitable, I guess, after the owners bailed on her."

"We had some great times there, didn't we?"

The words slipped out before he could stop them. Damned memory lane and the potholes he couldn't manage to swerve around, even in his mind.

Sofía's chest rose and fell on a heavy sigh. She ducked her head, her curtain of black hair draping to shield her face.

The urge to reach out and tuck her hair behind her ear, cup her cheek, lean in for a kiss, was stronger than his need to breathe. But he didn't have the right to do that anymore.

She'd taken that away from him when she'd asked him not to contact her again.

Right after his engagement with Melanie had hit the business news ticker.

"Yeah, we did, but—" With her trademark hair toss, Sofía straightened to stare back at him. Determination sparked in the golden hazel depths of her eyes. "But that's in the past. And it does no good to go there. Not for me anyway."

"Always looking ahead, aren't you? Eyes on the prize," he answered.

When it came to her career, she'd been laser-focused since they'd started college—him at Harvard, her at the University of Florida. Their first spring break, she'd planned to spend the week working on summer internship applications. He'd had to practically drag her to Daytona Beach for a few days of fun together.

"That's me. No rest for the weary," she countered.

The heavy note in her voice drew Nate's attention away from the property's *for-sale* sign.

Several cars made their slow drive past them, probably tourists cruising the main drag, peering in the windows at the wares and offerings in the tiny shops and businesses. The chime of a biker's bell tinkled a greeting, and the rider rolled by them.

But Nate's focus stayed on Sofía and the faint circles shadowing the skin under her expressive eyes.

Despite the "back-off" vibe her stiff posture exuded, he knew her well enough to tell that something was wrong. If there was one thing he'd never been able to ignore when it came to Sofía Vargas, it was his desire to always look out for her. Put her needs before his. Even if that need was a distance he didn't want.

"Are you doing okay?" He placed a comforting hand on

her forearm. "You want my help with—"

"No! I'm good." She took a hasty step back, and Nate let his hand fall at his side. "Look, I gotta go. I'm meeting the girls at Scallywags in a few. Good luck in Sarasota."

She slipped past him, ready to walk out of his life. Again.

"Hey," he called.

She turned around, one eyebrow arched in question.

"Tell Evie, Lauren, Jenna, and Lily I said hello," Nate offered. "I hope they're doing well."

A pained expression passed over Sofía's face. Her lips opened and closed as if she struggled for words. When she finally spoke, her voice was a husky whisper. "Thanks, I-I'll pass that along."

He watched her walk away, her shapely legs eating the distance between her and the friends who were more like family to her. For those two summers he and Sofía had shared here, he'd been a part of the Fabulous Five-some's insider group. Beachside picnics, bike rides, and sand volleyball games.

"Nate. Hey, Nate!" Tyson Braddock's call tugged Nate away from his remember-whens.

Across the street, Braddock stood in front of the JavaStop, right arm raised in greeting. Dressed in khaki slacks and a short-sleeved Oxford, with a pair of polished penny loafers, the guy hadn't changed much since they'd been at Harvard together. Based on the cheek-splitting grin on his face, Braddock appeared just as eager to get on Nate's good side, still determined to run with the "in" crowd.

Nate flicked one last glance in Sofía's direction. By now, she'd followed the curve onto Dock Street, the flash of her light purple sundress barely visible in the distance.

With a shake of his head, Nate turned back to the JavaStop and the business at hand.

If all went well, he'd close this deal quickly and be on his way.

Thoughts of Sofía Vargas and what could have been finally relegated to the past.

Reaching Braddock, Nate held out his hand in greeting. "Thanks for meeting me this afternoon. I'm looking forward to working with you."

The worried frown creasing Braddock's brow clued Nate in that the situation might not be as simple as he'd thought. The commissioner's next words confirmed it. "Actually, there's been a development since we spoke earlier this week. Looks like there's another party interested in bidding on the property, but I haven't gotten all the details yet."

Chapter Two

"SO, ARE YOU going to tell me what's got you simmering like a pressure cooker ready to blow, or am I going to have to pry it out of you?"

Sofía eyed Evie over the rim of her glass as she sipped her Don Q rum and Diet Coke.

Evie tucked her chin, her inquisitive blue eyes boring into Sofía. Unfortunately, Sofía knew that look. It was the same one her friend expertly wielded on the set of her talk show in Philly, especially when interviewing someone with a secret to hide.

Like Sofía did right now.

They'd been at Scallywags for about twenty minutes, and Lauren had excused herself to run to the bathroom near the entrance. That left Sofía and Evie to hold down their table while they waited for Jenna and her mystery boyfriend to arrive.

Stalling for time, Sofía jiggled the ice in her glass as she set it back on the scarred wooden table.

Evie raised both brows, lines creasing her normally smooth forehead. Her *"I-mean-business"* expression in full force.

Chickening out under the blatant stare down, Sofía slid her gaze around the bar. It was a Wednesday evening in April, so the place was pretty empty. Old man Nelson Dowler sat on a stool chatting with the friendly bartender Delilah, drowning his sorrows, as usual. Thankfully, he was a friendly drinker who never caused trouble.

A group of college kids filled two tables along the left side of the room, and an older couple took up a table for two in front of the wall of windows overlooking the ocean. Outside, dusk painted a kaleidoscope of purples, burnt oranges, and reds across the sky.

"Sooner or later, you're going to give in and 'fess up. You know that, right?" Evie pressed.

Yeah, she did.

But for now, with her insides still quaking, her heart stupidly fluttering at the sight of Nate, Sofía didn't want to talk about it. Couldn't.

Not without the fear of getting all teary, and she'd cried enough this weekend already. If she shed any more tears, it was dear sweet Lily who deserved them, not the man who hadn't been strong enough to stand up for himself. For them.

A man who hadn't wanted her enough to do so.

The door to the ladies' room swung open, and Lauren walked out. She smiled and waved, the cavalry coming back to save Sofía from spilling her guts in the middle of the town watering hole, though Lauren had no idea.

Sofía released the breath she hadn't realized she'd been holding, only to suck it back in with a gasp when Nate walked into Scallywags.

For a few seconds, it was like someone had snapped their fingers to make everyone freeze.

Standing in the entry near him, Lauren gaped at Nate, her pink lips open in an "Oh" of surprise.

"No freaking way," Evie muttered, slamming her gin and tonic down with a thud.

Ever the marketing and publicity pro capable of sizing up a situation and expertly switching into damage control mode, Lauren quickly recovered. She sent Nate an icy "*back-off*" glare before making a fast bee-line toward the girls' table in the back left corner.

"Where and when did you run into him before you got here?" Evie asked. "And don't bother denying you've already spoken to him. I could tell the moment you arrived that something was off."

"What the hell is Nate Hamilton doing in Paradise Key?" Lauren stage whispered as soon as she reached their table.

She fell into the chair next to Sofía, who couldn't resist tracking Nate to see his reaction to Lauren's cold shoulder.

With nothing but a chin jut of greeting in her general direction, Nate strolled over to an empty bar stool.

"It doesn't matter why he's here. What matters is that he stays away from Sof. And you..." Evie reached her arm out toward Sofía, then tapped the table top between them with her pointer finger. "You're better off without him. Right?"

"God yes, she's better off," Lauren answered for her, punctuating her proclamation with a scoff. "He's always been a player. More interested in good times and spending his daddy's money. You deserve better, Sof."

Yes, she did.

Only, the Nate she'd known was more than Lauren's description of him. Sure, the fun-loving rich kid antics of his youth were what most people remembered, but she'd been privy to so much more. His keen business mind, his disappointment when his father discounted his efforts, and his fiercely protective streak when it came to those in his inner circle. For a while there, she'd thought that maybe, one day…

Sofía shook her head, refusing to go there.

Foolish dreams she'd deluded herself into imagining. Though at least she'd only done so in the dark of night when it was just her and her thoughts.

"Come on, spill it," Evie urged.

"I ran into him in front of the JavaStop on my way over here," Sofía finally admitted. "Actually, across the street in front of the resort."

"And?" Evie pressed when she didn't continue.

Sofía traced a drop of condensation down the side of her glass, forcing the excited jitters to quiet.

And he'd looked heart-stompingly gorgeous with those chiseled cheekbones and strong jaw her Tía Mili used to say belonged on a telenovela actor. He'd also seemed tired. Dark circles under his green eyes. There'd been a strange mix of melancholy and anger around him. Though what he had to be angry about when it came to her, she had no idea.

Nor did she care to ask.

They were ancient history as far as she was concerned.

"And he said he was killing time before heading to Sarasota for business." Sofía took a long drink of her rum and Diet Coke.

"Hmph, well, he can kill time in some other town. Not ours." Lauren raised her glass to clink with Evie.

The door opened again, drawing their attention. This time a pair of welcomed guests entered, greeted with excited squeals from Sofía, Evie, and Lauren.

Jenna grinned as soon as she caught sight of them. She waved one hand, the other clasped with that of a tall, shaggy-haired guy who had a definite surfer vibe going on.

Evie jumped out of her seat, running to throw her arms around Jenna. Then she hooked arms with Jenna and the boyfriend they'd all been anxious to meet, ushering the pair to their table.

Once again that inquisitive look sparkled in Evie's blue eyes. A spurt of empathy wormed its way through Sofía's chest, followed closely by relief that she was off the interview hot seat. For now, at least.

Nate watched Sofía, her girlfriends, and some guy he didn't know chatting at the round-top table. Occasionally, there was laughter. Once or twice, he caught one of the girls swiping away a tear.

He shifted on his bar stool, nursing a glass of Michter's 10 Year Single Barrel Bourbon, itching to go over and offer his condolences.

God, he felt like a complete jerk. Not that he should have been expected to know about Lily's accident. Sure, at one time, Sofía would have called him to talk about it. Not anymore, though.

Tyson Braddock had seen him talking with Sofía earlier, and assumed she'd told Nate about the funeral services that had taken place this past weekend.

Nate took a sip of his drink, focusing on the slow burn trickling down his throat. As crappy as things might have been lately, at least he was here. It was hard to grasp the idea that one of Sofía's Fabulous Five-some was actually gone. Those girls were her sisters, by choice if not by blood. Losing one had to have hit Sofía hard.

Family meant everything to her. It was why she'd been so determined to graduate from college, making her parents proud as she represented the first in their family to earn a degree.

It was also why she'd balked every time Nate had intentionally done something to stick it to his father during their summers working at the resort in high school. She used to lecture him on the importance of *familia*.

Funny though, by the end of their first year of college, she'd stopped harping on him about finding a way to make peace with his old man. As if somehow, she'd realized peaceful wasn't an adjective anyone would use with Nathan Patrick Hamilton, II.

Footsteps approached, and Nate glanced up to find Evie Barclay sauntering over. With her lips pursed in a haughty expression, he knew she wasn't coming over for a social call. Years ago, Nate's father and Evie's had been golfing buddies when the two were in Florida.

"Evie," he greeted, saluting her with his tumbler. "How's your dad doing?"

"I wouldn't know. Haven't talked to him in ages," she answered. "Which is what Sofía needs to continue saying about you."

"I'm sure Sofía can speak for herself."

"We both know she can. But I'm telling you to stay away. She's got something good going now, and I won't let you screw that up because you wanna fool around."

"Still playing hard ball, aren't you?" Nate shot back. Ridiculous anger simmered in his belly. Of course Sofía had moved on and found someone else. Why wouldn't she?

Evie glanced over her shoulder at their table.

Nate followed her gaze to find Sofía frowning in their direction.

"Look," Evie said, turning to face him again. She

combed a hand through her blonde waves, then fisted it on her hip. "You and I both grew up with crappy fathers who think throwing money and their weight around gets them what they want. Sofía doesn't operate like that. She's worked hard for what she has, and she doesn't deserve to be played. By anyone. I don't know why you're really in Paradise Key, but whatever it is, wrap it up fast and move on."

"That's the plan," Nate answered.

"Good. Nice chatting with you." Before he could say anything else, Evie spun on her sandaled feet, heading for the ladies' room.

Nate downed the rest of his whiskey, dug a twenty-dollar bill out of his wallet, then dropped it on the bar top. So much for going over to offer his condolences. None of those ladies wanted to hear it from him. He wasn't their friend. Not really even Evie's, despite their old family tie.

He shouldn't want to comfort Sofía, especially since she was the one who'd cut him loose.

Still, he couldn't resist one last glance in her direction.

Head angled to the side, exposing the smooth column of her throat, she listened intently to whatever story Jenna and the surfer guy she'd walked in with were telling the rest of the girls. Sofía's almond-shaped eyes crinkled with pleasure, her full lips tilting up in a gentle smile.

As if she felt his gaze on her, she shifted, looking over her shoulder at him. Her mouth thinned, the beauty mark above the right corner drawing his attention while the sparkle faded from her eyes.

The guarded expression blanketing her classic features twisted his insides. Reminded him of the distance she'd chosen to put between them. And the pain he'd tried to mask by burying himself in work and proving himself to his father.

Without another word, Nate turned to leave. He wasn't here for a reunion, and he didn't need any distractions.

Tomorrow he was meeting with the vice chair of the Local Planning Agency to tour the resort. Supposedly the other interested party would be there as well.

It'd be the perfect opportunity to size up his competition. Then he'd get busy figuring out the best way to beat them.

Chapter Three

"*A DIOS,* TÍA MILI, I'll see you later today," Sofía called to her aunt midmorning on Friday.

"Wait! *¿Comiste algo, nena?*" Tía Milagros hurried out from the kitchen, wiping her hands with a blue towel.

"*Sí,* I ate something while you were in the shower."

Tía Milagros shot her the arched brow "*don't-try-to-pull-a-fast-one-on-me*" stare that mothers the world over managed to master. Even though Tía Mili hadn't raised kids of her own, she'd been Sofía's de facto parent every summer from the age of ten through high school.

Hand on the doorknob, Sofía paused, barely holding back a beleaguered sigh. It didn't matter that she was thirty and not thirteen; she'd always be a young girl in her *tía's* eyes. And respect for *familia* had been ingrained in Sofía since baptism.

"I had cafe con leche with a boiled egg, so I'm good to go."

Tía Mili huffed. "*Ay nena,* you eat like a *pajarito.* If you're not careful, you'll blow away in the wind."

Sofía chuckled, hurrying over to press a kiss on her *tía's* cheek. "*Bueno,* this little bird has to fly the coop. I'm meeting Vida Mayfair at Paradise Key Resort for a walk-through. I'll grab something at Deli 2983 if I get hungry."

"I am so proud of you, *nena*." Tía Mili gave her a tight hug, the crisp scent of pine cleaner filling Sofía's lungs. "You are such a good example for your brothers. Always working hard. Helping others, like me, to reach for our dreams. I am praying very hard for this to work out for you."

"*Gracias, tía.*" After another quick squeeze, Sofía slipped out the front door of her *tía's* modest two-bedroom condo.

She hurried down the three flights of rickety wooden steps. Reaching the bottom, she sidestepped one of the thick-beamed stilts that lifted the wood-slat building high off the ground to avoid potential flooding during hurricane season. Her *tía* had lived in this same ten-unit complex, barely a five-minute walk down Old Mill Drive and 2nd Street to the resort, since she and Tío David had moved here from Miami nearly twenty-five years ago.

Both had landed jobs at the resort. Tía Mili in housekeeping; Tío David in maintenance. They had carved out a new life on this quiet little beach island, away from the hectic city life. Sofía had loved family visits to see her favorite *tía* and *tío*. But three short years into their idyllic life here, Tío David had drowned in a freak boating accident. Mami had thought her sister would move back to Miami with them, or to Puerto Rico with the rest of the *familia*.

But Mili had stayed, clinging to the memories she and her beloved had created in Paradise Key. That next summer, at the age of ten, Sofía had begged to stay with Tía Mili instead of going to her abuela's in Puerto Rico.

"I can keep her company. And then she won't be so lonely," she had pleaded with Mami and Papi.

That had been Sofía's first full summer in Paradise Key. She'd come here wanting to be close to her *tía*, offer her comfort. Not knowing her life would change when she met Jenna and Lily at a local arts festival, then later connected with Evie and Lauren while sneaking a dip in the resort pool one blazingly hot and humid July afternoon.

Sofía hefted her laptop satchel higher on her shoulder, then glanced at her slim gold watch. It was nine forty. She wasn't meeting Vida until ten. Plenty of time for her to slow her walk and mentally review the notes and questions she'd put together in preparation.

Out on the Gulf, a fishing boat headed for deeper water. The sun glistened off the rippling blue surface, white flumes spraying in the boat's wake. The tranquility of the ocean with the horizon just out of reach never failed to calm her.

A few cars moseyed their way down 2nd Street, either locals or tourists who'd adopted the island's slow pace of life. A pair of teenaged bikers on beach cruisers pedaled by with smiles and waves for her. Up ahead on the sidewalk, a mom with two little kids underfoot tugged open the door to Delightful Scoops. One of the shaggy-haired youngsters whooped with an excited, "I'm getting cookies and cream, okay, Mom?"

Sofía grinned at his exuberance, then craned her neck to check both ways before stepping into the road to cross to the property.

She reached the parking lot, her sandaled feet slowing when she noticed two cars parked near the resort's arching entry. One was a dark green convertible with Georgia license plates. The other was an old Ford truck that, based on the Levy County, Florida, tag and the "Paradise Key, Best Place to Be" bumper sticker, no doubt belonged to Vida. Born and raised on the island, the older woman was one of the biggest proponents for keeping growth in check to avoid altering the family friendly, nature-loving vibe.

Sofía was counting on Vida's strong sentiments to carry over into what the older woman envisioned for the resort. That would play right into Sofía's idea to turn it into a family vacation, nature-themed destination wedding site.

Wondering who might have joined Vida before Sofía's arrival, she hurried up the tile walkway toward the glass revolving door.

Her heart dive-bombed into her stomach, then ricocheted up to lodge in her throat when she spotted Nate, elbow bent as he leaned against the registration desk off to the left. Looking comfortably casual in khaki pants and a striped navy and light blue button-down shirt, he straightened as soon as he saw her. His brows slanted in a confused scowl.

"There she is," Vida greeted her with gusto as soon as the

revolving door spit Sofía into the lobby.

The older woman clapped her hands, glee brightening her lined features. Gray curls framed her face like a metallic bike helmet, the perfect foil for her bright blue eyes. Her baggy jeans, loose-fitting floral blouse, and Birkenstock sandals rounded out Vida's child-of-the-sixties look, her friendly personality a welcome accessory.

Vida rushed over to give Sofía a hug in greeting, then stepped back to stretch an arm out toward Nate as she announced, "Well, now that you've both arrived, we can get started with the tour."

"Wait, why is he here?" Sofía asked, pointing at Nate.

"Excuse me?" he said at the same time.

They both broke off, his annoyed glare answering the one she aimed his way.

"Oh dear, I thought Tyson would have told you. Or did he ask me to do that?" Vida pressed a knuckle to her pursed lips. "No, I'm pretty sure he said he'd handle that. Maybe? Anyway..." She waved off the issue like it didn't matter. "I figured since the two of you go way back, you wouldn't mind doing this together. That way I can be sure to share the same information with you, since you're both potential bidders."

Sofía flinched at Vida's words. "I hadn't realized there *was* another interested party. Tyson—" the slime ball, "—neglected to mention that when I first spoke with him on Monday."

"My people have been looking into this property for several weeks now," Nate said, his aloof tone indicating she was the interloper here. "Braddock and I have spoken multiple times. The first I heard of another interested party was Wednesday, when he and I met for coffee. But he didn't say who it was."

Sofía bit back an exasperated groan. Of course his "people" were involved. That also meant the Hamilton name, money, and reputation. Braddock, social-climber extraordinaire, was probably lapping up the chance to rub elbows with Nate. Just like the schmoozer had done when the two men had been at Harvard.

Her stomach clenched with disappointment.

Dios mío, she'd been banking on her bid being the only one. That would make it difficult for anyone on the Local Planning Agency, even Braddock who was the LPA's chair, to turn her down and risk keeping the resort in its current state of disrepair. An eyesore for the community. With the LPA on her side, odds were better the local bank might approve her loan, despite her shaky financial situation.

"I'm fine doing this together. Hamilton Inc. has nothing to hide." Hands in the front pockets of his khaki slacks, Nate struck a nonchalant pose. He flashed the infamous Hamilton smile he'd inherited from his father. The teeth-baring, confident one that typically won over doubters and fans alike.

Like Vida, who grinned back at him.

But Sofía knew Nate well enough to note the slight tightening of his square jaw when he focused her way. The flash of challenge in his eyes irked her. Even with his mother's green eyes, Nate resembled his father far too much. The Hamilton competitive streak that could turn ugly on a dime wasn't something she'd seen often in Nate. If anything, he'd sought to be different, despising his father's ruthlessness.

Apparently, things had changed in the two years since she'd cut off communication with him.

Bueno, she had changed, too. Her career goals were now in sharper focus. Nothing, and no one, would stand in her way of winning this bid.

"Oh, I'm good with it, too." Sofía quirked a shoulder, pretending she didn't have a care in the world. "Let Nate get a look at the property as it is now, that way when he comes back for the grand re-opening, he'll appreciate my vision even more."

Vida threw back her head with a cackle.

Nate's lips twitched like he was fighting off his own laugh.

Sofía smiled, the crack in his Hamilton veneer warming the chill between them.

"Cheeky girl. I've always told Mili that I liked your gumption," Vida said on a chuckle. "Smart advice you gave her about starting her own cleaning company before this place shut down."

"Thanks," Sofía answered, surprised Vida knew about

her role in guiding Tía Mili through the steps of becoming a small business owner. Then again, there were few secrets in a town of this size, especially since the two ladies regularly volunteered at church together. "I'm relieved things are going well for her."

"Me too." Vida rubbed Sofía's upper arm in a friendly gesture that spoke of their personal connection.

Sofía felt Nate's intuitive gaze on them. Probably calculating how that personal connection might play into the Local Planning Agency's decision.

To her count, it was one vote for each of them because more than likely Nate had Braddock's wrapped up. Sofía was crossing her fingers she'd have Vida's. Not because of their relationship, but because Sofía was confident she understood what the long-time locals wanted for their community. No way the Hamiltons had their finger on the pulse of this town like she did. Money could only buy so much.

"Okay then." Vida swung her gaze from Sofía to Nate. "Let's get this party started, shall we?"

"Lead the way." Nate gave a gentlemanly tilt of his head, indicating he'd follow behind them.

The older woman began regaling them with details about the property, how it had changed hands several times since Nate's family had sold the resort about seven years ago. After the last owners had closed the doors and left town without warning, alerting their employees via email, the city had bought the property. The goal now was to find the right owners, with the right restoration plan and ideas to fit the island's vision for its future.

As they walked through the bare lobby area, the tile floor faded and cracked in places, nostalgia lingered in the air, filling Sofía's lungs with every breath. If she closed her eyes, she could picture the place as it had been in its heyday. Tía Mili in her peach-colored uniform dress, pushing her cart down the carpeted hallways in the main building or between the private cabanas along the left side of the lush property. Lauren and Evie hanging out by the pool, waiting for Sofía to finish her shift at the Tiki Hut grill. Lily and Jenna showing up when they finished their local part-time jobs, too. Nate standing behind the registration desk in a polo bearing the Hamilton swirling "H" logo, heading out to the pool area so they could meet up during their breaks.

Good times. Innocent times.

She'd known it would probably end when they all went away to college. Sofía simply hadn't counted on the hateful role Nate's dad had tried to play in it. The audacity of that man tracking her down on campus, trying to bribe her with money for college if she'd quit "distracting" Nate from his responsibilities.

Por favor, she had ripped his check in half and, head held high, walked away. Never telling anyone about the one and only time she'd exchanged private words with the cretin. It was a secret she'd even kept from Nate, more to salvage her own pride than to protect his bully of a father.

Shaking off the hateful memory, Sofía keyed back into Vida's tale of the resort's recent history. Twenty minutes into their tour, when they'd only hit the lobby and dining room, Vida's cell chimed an incoming call from the back pocket of her baggy jeans. She fished it out, excusing herself as soon as she realized it was her husband.

Vida moved a few feet away for privacy. It wasn't far enough away for Nate and Sofía not to catch the older woman's shocked gasp. "Orville, what do you mean you may or may not need stitches? How bad is it?"

Sofía exchanged a surprised look with Nate. Both stepped closer when Vida visibly paled.

"Good Lord. Sit tight. I'll be home in less than five. And prepare yourself. If I say we're going to the emergency room, we're going."

A deep grumble could be heard before Vida disconnected the call.

"Everything okay with Orville?" Sofía asked, mentally thunking herself on the back of the head for the inane question. Obviously, there was a problem.

"Word to the wise, sweetie, when you encourage your newly retired husband to pick up a hobby, make sure it's not one that involves sharp objects, okay?" Vida heaved a disgruntled sigh as she shook her head.

"Men—can't live with 'em, can't shoot 'em," Sofía offered in commiseration. She gave Nate a side-eye glare that had Vida laughing and him pshaw-ing.

"Something like that." Vida fished a set of keys from her front pocket. "Look, if I leave these with you two, will you promise to lock her up tight and get them back to me by tomorrow? I can't imagine anyone would have a problem with you being here. It's not like you're strangers or anything."

Sofía flinched. Continue the walk-through with Nate, alone?

The emotional side of her brain told her to follow Vida out the revolving door.

The business side reminded her she needed to get a lay of the land to better strengthen some of the points in her bid.

"Sure." Nate took the keys from Vida. "I don't mind dropping them off. Don't worry about us. Go see what your husband needs. We're good. Right, Sofía?"

The worry in Vida's normally bright blue eyes tipped the scales of Sofía's indecision. "Yeah, you go take care of Orville. Let me know if there's anything Tía Mili or I can do to help."

She gave Vida a hug good-bye, then watched her family friend hurry out.

"Just you and me, like old times, huh?"

Nate's off-the-cuff remark was like the flame from a tiki torch reigniting her anger and frustration.

Sofía rounded on him in a flash of indignation. "Do you really have business in Sarasota, Nate? Was that even the truth? Or was it more of that infamous Hamilton shark-like strategy? That's where we are now, huh? You lying to my face?"

He reared back, brows raised in surprise.

When he opened his mouth to respond, she threw up a hand in a stop sign. "Forget it. It doesn't matter anyway."

She was too overwhelmed by emotion, too near the edge of tears she absolutely refused to cry in front of him. God forbid he'd think she was crying over him, and not the very real threat of losing her dream before she'd even had a chance to savor the potential.

Her throat crammed with heartache, Sofía spun away, ready to head off on her own solo tour of the resort.

Nate grabbed her wrist, stopping her.

"Don't," he said, his voice gruff with an emotion she couldn't place. "Don't walk away like this. Not again. Please."

That last word got to her.

Jerky. Haughty. Domineering. All of those Hamilton traits she could easily turn her back on, giving him the finger on her way out.

But humble contrition laced with a ribbon of pain echoed in his pinched expression, ensnaring her as securely as one of Tío David's or her papi's fishing hooks.

Swallowing the hurt, but grabbing onto her anger, Sofía turned back to face Nate. "Fine. What do you have to say for yourself?"

Chapter Four

WHAT DO YOU *have to say for yourself?*

Sofía's question was eerily close to the one his father had thrown at him when he'd stormed into Nate's office last week, still pissed about Nate and Melanie's broken engagement.

Forget that thirty minutes earlier, Nate had forwarded his dad an email about two smaller prospective properties Nate had researched and made on-site visits to over the past several months. Both hotels were nearly in the bag, key acquisitions in his plan to form a small conglomerate of boutique resorts within Hamilton, Inc.; a division Nate sought to manage, if his father would ever give him the green light.

Foolishly, Nate had expected a congratulatory toast with the bottle of Pappy Van Winkle whiskey his father kept in his office. But Nathan Hamilton, II, didn't want to listen to business plans involving luxury boutique hotels. Not when he'd rather berate Nate over his inability to close the simplest of mergers. Namely, marriage to a woman who'd always been a friend, never a lover.

The last thing his father wanted to hear was Nate expressing his thanks for Melanie's ability to see the light first. Saving them both from making a grave mistake.

So, the senior Hamilton had responded in the only way he knew how. Banishing Nate once more to the sedate beaches of Paradise Key. It was his dad's way of testing him. Using his rapier-sharp tongue to slash at Nate's pride with the claim that maybe he wasn't ready to be trusted with the family business. The same edict he'd given the summer when Nate was first ordered to the island fourteen years ago.

To sixteen-year-old Nate, being relegated to this sleepy island town had been like a prison sentence. The opposite of working at their Atlantic City property, closer to his friends.

Then Sofía had walked through the revolving glass doors, and, just like it did now, his pulse raced with anticipation.

Thunderstruck.

That was the best way to describe how he'd felt back then. And today.

Seeing her push through the main doors a little while ago… Finding out she was the competition for a deal he could not afford to lose…

Irony of freaking ironies. He'd thought being back here, seeing her with her friends and knowing she'd easily moved on without him, was as bad as it could get.

Sofía glared at his hand, still holding onto her wrist, then up at him. The gold flecks in her hazel eyes flashed with irritation, her sandal tapping the tile floor as she waited for his explanation.

He released her, shoving his hands in his pockets to keep from reaching out for her again.

"Look, I didn't lie to you. Not exactly," he amended when she sucked her teeth in derision.

"You're splitting hairs, and you know it." She folded her arms across her chest, right hip cocked in a sassy jut that made the conservative, short-sleeved pencil dress she wore temptingly sexy. "I've told you before, a lie of omission is equally as bad."

Feisty, but moral, that was his Sofía.

Only she wasn't his.

Squelching a spurt of disappointment, Nate forced his mind back to business. "There *is* a property down in Sarasota we're interested in. If things don't pan out here."

Her full lips tightened, like she was struggling to keep words from spilling out.

"I didn't say anything when we ran into each other the other day because I didn't think it would matter," Nate continued. "And, honestly, because it's too early in the game."

"Right. 'Cuz this…" She opened her arms to encompass the open lobby area and expansive dining hall, gesturing toward the elevator bank that led to the standard rooms off to the right. "This is all a game to you. To Hamilton, Inc., it's another property in a long string of them. But it's not a game, Nate. This place means a lot to me. And to my *tía.*"

"I know."

"Then don't bid."

Indecision flashed across her face as soon as she said the words. If she could take them back, he'd bet she would.

"You don't mean that, Sof." He shook his head, knowing her and her competitive streak. That chip on her shoulder, figuratively and literally thanks to her tattoo, drove her to succeed. "When it comes to your work, you wouldn't roll over for someone else any more than you'd expect me to. As much as you want this place, I think you'd regret asking me to back out and you not fighting for it."

Sofía's face scrunched in a grimace, but it did nothing to detract from her beauty.

"*Coño.*" She grumbled the Spanish curse word under her breath, repeating the "damn" once more. "You're probably right."

She spun away, striding a few steps toward the dining hall before quickly turning back to point at him. "But mark my words, I'm going to win this bid fair and square. The important question is can I count on Hamilton Inc.—can I count on *you* and your father—to do the same?"

Nate's chest tightened with a burning mix of anger and pain. How could she even ask him that question? Worse, how could she so easily group him in with his old man when she knew how much Nate detested his father's strong-arm tactics?

"Are you serious?" he ground out.

Sofía's determined expression was answer enough.

"That's a low blow," he muttered.

The disquiet simmering inside him lately heated to a slow boil. Nate stabbed his fingers through his hair in frustration.

This past weekend, trying to avoid another argument with his father, Nate had canceled dinner plans with his parents. The next morning, his mom showed up at his place. Worry clouding her green eyes, she carried a white paper bag from his favorite bakery in one hand and a tray with two cups of coffee in the other.

It didn't matter that her conciliatory gesture should have come from her husband. Yeah, right. Like that would ever happen. As usual, Nate had promised his mom that he'd toe the Hamilton line. Pacify his dad to keep the family peace.

Of course, he hadn't known at the time that handling the reacquisition of Paradise Key Resort meant he'd be battling Sofía for the bid. A promise to his mom was a promise he couldn't break, but what if it meant hurting the only other woman he'd cared for as much as her?

Talk about being stuck between a rock and a hard place.

"This isn't personal, Sofía." He couldn't allow it to be.

"It's personal to me. And you didn't answer my question," she pressed.

"Yes, you have my word. No back-door deals." He could give her that at least. The promise he wouldn't let his father play dirty.

"Thank you." She bobbed her head in a brisk nod.

"In all honesty, you're the one who'd have better access to the back doors of most Paradise Key residents. Not me."

"Maybe." She hitched a shoulder in a blasé shrug. "But Tyson Braddock has wanted inside your circle for years. I'm sure he's salivating at the chance to help you and your father so he can get in your good graces."

Nate waved off her argument. "The guy's not all that bad. From what I can tell, he seems to want what's best for the town."

"I sure hope so." Sofía made a slow circle, taking in the interior's shabby condition. As quickly as it had flashed, her ire slipped away. Nostalgia softened her expression when she faced him. "She deserves to be resurrected, doesn't she?"

"Yeah, she does, even if it's only for the town's sake."

Sofía's gaze caught with his. A hushed silence fell between them, weighed down by thoughts of what was and what could have been.

There were a lot of good memories here—his own with Sofía, but also those of countless guests who had vacationed here and the locals who'd been on the payroll during the resort's heyday.

It would be good to see the property up and running, flourishing again.

His phone vibrated in his front pocket, breaking the delicate thread linking them.

Sofía glanced away, and Nate reached for his cell to check the caller ID. His father's name flashed across the screen, a glaring reminder of Nate's duty to his family. He pressed the button to send the call directly to voicemail.

"We should probably finish the tour and get out of here," Nate said.

Sofía twisted her wrist to check her watch. "Yes, I've got a phone call in a little over an hour."

Nate couldn't help but wonder if the call was for business or pleasure.

He should only be interested in the first, and how it might tie into her bid on the property. But the jealous whispers inside his head wondering about the second wouldn't be silenced. Evie had told him Sofía had a good thing going now. Damn if he didn't want to know with whom. And how serious it might be.

Shaking off the distracting questions, Nate stepped toward the elevator bank.

"You good with starting inside, then heading to check the grounds and cabanas after? I've heard some of them have a bit of hurricane damage."

"Sure." Sofía fell into step beside him, and he caught the faint whiff of her spicy floral perfume.

The scent infused his body like a hallucinogenic drug, eliciting a vivid image that flashed in his mind. Her dark hair fanning out on her pillow beside him, a silky contrast to the cream-colored sheets in the hotel room they'd shared in Key West the last time they'd been together.

Damn, he'd lost track of the number of nights he'd lain

awake in bed, reliving that weekend. With her, he felt rejuvenated, uplifted, capable of anything.

It'd been a glorious weekend, right up until the moment he finally revealed his father's latest edict: Put a ring on Melanie Brokaw's finger and officially unite the two families, as expected.

"Why is Hamilton, Inc., interested in the resort now?" Sofía's question broke into Nate's musings.

"I don't think we should have let it go to begin with," he answered. "Remember, you and I were still in college when the decision was made to sell it and invest in another property."

The silver elevator door slid open, and he waited for Sofía to enter first.

"Any preference?" She waved at the panel of circular numbered lights. He shook his head, so she pressed the number three. "It was Tía Mili's floor when she worked here."

"How is she?" Nate asked, remembering with fondness the slender woman with a strong work ethic and friendly personality. Sofía and her *tía* shared the same golden hazel eyes, generous smile, and devotion to their family. Nate envied their close connection. Knowing someone was always in your corner, no matter what.

For a while, he'd had that with Sofía. Until he'd blown it.

The elevator creaked its way upward. She leaned her

right shoulder against the wall, her gaze trained on the circles as they lit up. "Tía Mili's good, thanks for asking."

"She still making that killer roast pork and Puerto Rican rice?"

Sofía chuckled as she patted her trim belly. "Better than ever. That's why I've increased my run distance since I've been here."

There'd been a time when Nate would have teased her about another way they could work off a few calories together. Now he wisely kept that idea to himself.

"I always liked hanging out at her house," he said instead, remembering those summer evenings with fondness. The ease with which Tía Mili had welcomed him, participating in their conversations. Listening without judging. "It felt homey and comfortable. Accepting."

"That's *familia*."

"Well, your *familia* maybe. Mine hasn't quite grasped the 'fun' part of dysfunctional."

Sofía's brows hitched lower and she started to respond, but the elevator slid to a stop.

"Come on, let's see what we're buying," he said, gesturing for her to go ahead again.

"Correction, what *I'm* buying."

Nate shook his head at the smirk she tossed him on her way out. "Smart aleck," he teased.

She answered with a quirked brow he found entirely too sexy.

Together, they wandered the hall, remarking on the stained carpeting, checking out a few rooms to survey the conditions, poking at the edges of peeling wallpaper in one. Sofía whipped out a small spiral notebook and pen from the brown satchel slung over her shoulder.

He watched her take notes, barely curbing his curiosity's desire for him to step closer and read over her shoulder. Not that she would have let him anyway.

She was all business. Intently focused on achieving her goal. Just like he needed to be.

"The pictures I've seen didn't do the damage justice," Nate said.

Sofía shook her head as she jotted in her notebook. "Definitely not."

He snapped a few photos with his phone, then typed his own list into a document he'd email to himself once they were finished.

Soon, they were going back down in the elevator, crossing the cracked tile floor toward the sliding glass doors leading outside.

A humid ocean breeze greeted them. Palm trees and oleander bushes with dark pink buds dotted the overgrown grounds. Thick weeds choked the colorful foliage, clamoring for dominance until they reached the edge of the sandy beach. The Tiki Hut restaurant appeared ready for hurricane season, its windows battened down, the chairs and tables stacked and tied together with heavy rope. The drained freeform-shaped pool and circular jacuzzi sat like gaping wounds in an area that had once been the resort's thriving, energetic heartbeat.

"Wow," Sofía whispered. "I haven't tried to come back here in years. It's…it's so sad."

Her voice was thick with emotion, and Nate found himself unable to resist wading into the waters of their shared memories.

"Remember that time you jumped in the pool to grab that toddler who'd fallen in?" he asked.

Sofía clapped a hand to her forehead. "*Dios mío*, I'd forgotten about that. The Tiki Hut shift manager was not happy I had to go home and change."

"Hell, it would have been worse if you'd stuck around looking like the winner of a wet T-shirt contest. Not that I woulda minded."

She elbowed him in the ribs, but the smile curving her full lips made the jab feel more like a love tap.

"That mom made sure the entire staff knew how grateful she was for your quick thinking," he added.

"It almost seems like yesterday," Sofía said, her eyes taking on a faraway haze as she moved closer to the edge of the pool.

Nate followed, surprised when she sank down to sit with her tanned legs dangling into what should have been the deep end. He joined her, tugging at his pant legs to sit comfortably at her side.

"The girls made such a big deal about it," she continued, lost in the memory as she stared into the cement shell. "Evie and Lauren hailed me a hero and queen for the rest of the day. Jenna wove a crown out of some twine, then glued on a bunch of shells from her grandmother's shop. And when we got to Delightful Scoops after my shift, Lily talked them into—"

Her voice hitched, and she broke off.

He caught the tremble of her chin, the pain of losing her dear friend obviously overwhelming her.

Eyes closed, Sofía hung her head. A curtain of her dark hair fell to shield her face from his view. Still, she couldn't hide the shudder that shook her thin shoulders when she sucked in a breath.

Nate could no more not offer her comfort than he could will his heart to stop beating. Instinctively, he wrapped his arm around her, guiding Sofía gently to his side.

He half expected her to pull away, rebuffing him like she'd done over the past two years. Instead, she surprised him by sinking into him and burying her face in his neck. Warm tears wet his skin as she cried.

"I'm so sorry about Lily," he murmured. "I had no idea yesterday when I asked you to tell her hello for me."

"I fi-figured as much," Sofía said in between another shuddering breath.

"Tyson Braddock mentioned it in passing. I wanted to say something when we were at Scallywags…but you all looked so happy together. I didn't want to interrupt with a reminder of bad news."

"It's hard," she whispered. "The only *familia* I've lost before was Tío David and my *abuela*. That was difficult enough. Yet, you don't think someone as young as Lily could, could be gone so—"

Her body shook with gut-wrenching sobs. Nate twisted, enveloping her in a tight embrace. Willing her pain to seep into him. God, he'd give anything to make it go away.

"I'm so sorry, Sof," he repeated, stroking a hand gently through her hair.

Little by little, her sobs subsided, slowing to a hiccupping breath. Sofía leaned away slightly, and Nate let his arms slide to rest on her hips.

She scrubbed at her eyes, leaving a trail of mascara on her fingers. "I shouldn't have—"

"Don't worry about it. That's what friends are for."

Her red-rimmed, puffy eyes narrowed. "Yeah, well, I'm not sure I'd call us 'friends' anymore."

"I would. Or at least I'd like to."

Honestly, he didn't know if he could *be* just friends with Sofía. They'd been more than that for years. An unlabeled, but important relationship in his life. Until she'd severed the tie saying they couldn't see each other anymore if he was engaged to another woman.

Could he be this close and not touch her? Was it possible for him to ignore the urge to kiss her senseless?

He wasn't sure, but friendship was a far better alternative than what he'd had with her over the last two years—complete silence.

"I'm not sure your fiancée would approve of you hanging out with an ex-lover," Sofía shot back, scrambling to her feet.

"If I had a fiancée, she might not. Seeing as I don't have one anymore, it's a moot point."

Sofía stared down at him, surprise flashing across her features. He knew she wanted to ask what had happened, but she wouldn't. Pride would keep her from doing so.

Nate pushed himself to a stand, wiping off the seat of his pants as he spoke. "Suffice to say that my dad's going to have to find another way to combine the Hamilton and Brokaw empires because a marriage between Melanie and me is not in the cards. It was a crazy stupid move to begin with."

"Well then, I guess my condolences or my congratulations are in order. Whichever you and Melanie prefer. That's between the two of you. Not us. Or rather, there is no 'us' so it doesn't really matter." Sofía's hands fluttered nervously in the air between them.

Strange, because he'd rarely seen her nervous. Calm and collected, sure. Pissed or emotionally charged, hell yeah. But nervous? Only when she'd *really* wanted that summer internship her first year of college. Maybe right before she'd gone for her interview with the small resort chain on South Beach after her graduation from the University of Florida.

He hoped it was a sign that she cared, and maybe there

was a chance, slim as it might be, that they could reconnect.

Taking a step toward her, he held out a hand. "Look, isn't it possible for us—"

"I can't do this, Nate. Not now." Sofía backed away, shaking her head from side to side so hard her hair swished like a dark cape behind her. "I have a plan, and it's a solid one. If I'm successful, *when* I'm successful, it will mean so much to me, and to my Tía Mili. It'll bring me home to the *familia* I have here in Paradise Key. And I can't let you, and certainly not your father and the unsavory methods he uses to deal with whatever or *whomever* is in his way, derail me."

Nate started at the vehemence in Sofía's voice, shocked and confused about where it came from. As far as he knew, Sofía and his dad had only met in passing that last summer in Paradise Key. How could she know anything about the way his old man did business, except for what Nate had griped about over the years?

"I have to go," Sofía said, interrupting Nate's mental debate.

"Wait!" He reached out to stop her. Damn it, he didn't want her to leave like this. Upset with him, hurting over Lily's death, and seeming almost angry with his dad for whatever strange reason.

Discouraged by the increasing distance between them, he sought to shorten it. "You know that if you need anything. Ever. Someone to talk to…"

"I'll call one of the girls." Sofía filled in the blank he'd left by letting his sentence trail off. "In fact, we're meeting at Jenna's later for a girls' night in, then tomorrow I'm heading down to St. Pete for an overnight with Lauren and Evie. We're grieving, but I'll be fine."

Of course she would. Because unlike him, she'd been okay with their breakup. If the end of a non-dating, occasional hookup relationship could be called a breakup.

"See you around, Nate." She raised a hand in a listless wave, giving him a wobbly smile that did nothing to hide the pain in her expressive eyes. "Take care."

"You too," he answered. His heart thudded painfully in his chest as she strode inside the resort without another glance back at him.

As soon as she was gone, Nate sank down at the pool's edge again. He jabbed a hand through his hair, shell-shocked at the scrambled mess his life had become.

His phone vibrated in his pocket, but he didn't have to check to know who was calling. He'd told his father about the walk-through. No doubt the old man was calling for a full report.

If Nate didn't answer, his father would assume the worst, that Nate had somehow messed up.

He let out a heavy sigh of resignation. Better to get the unpleasant conversation over with now. Then he could head back to the room he'd rented. Make a few calls that should provide info and figures that would benefit his official report on their bid. The rest of his afternoon, he planned to spend touching base with a few contacts in Sarasota before heading to Scallywags to grab a bite.

A tasty burger, a finger or two of smooth whiskey, and the picturesque Paradise Key sunset view. The perfect combination to fuel his brainstorm session as he figured out what the hell he was going to do about Sofía. If he'd somehow be able to convince her to give them another shot, or if standing on opposing sides of the city commission's vote would drive a wedge between them he'd never be able to dislodge.

Pulling out his cell, Nate tapped the green icon on the screen to answer the call. "Hello, Father. To what do I owe the honor?"

"Cut the crap," his dad's voice boomed through the speaker. "What the hell's going on down there?"

Chapter Five

"IT'S GREAT TO hear from you," Nate bit out the words, bristling at his father's propensity to micromanage him. Only when it came to business because, frankly, they spent very little time together outside of the office.

Nathan Hamilton, II, busied himself with networking, researching potential investments, or finagling an inside track on whatever deal he was either involved with or wanted in on. Idle conversation with his son about mundane topics like what was new in Nate's life or what his own goals might be didn't advance any of those pursuits. That meant it never occurred.

"I called earlier. Why didn't you pick up?" his father barked.

"Probably because I was in the middle of the walk-through. Which, had you looked at the office shared calendar, you would have been aware of."

Too keyed up to stay still, Nate hopped to his feet, striding along the perimeter of the free-form-shaped pool.

"So?"

"So what?" Oh, he knew what his father wanted. Perversely, Nate felt compelled to make him ask.

A huff of breath whooshed through the speaker.

"Nate, I don't have the time or the patience to deal with your games. What's your assessment of the property?"

"A lot of work to be done. The main building has some water damage from storm surges during past hurricane seasons. The grounds are pretty rough. Still have to check out the cabanas to get a clear picture."

No need to admit he'd gotten a little side tracked by Sofía and his compulsion to be with her, to offer her comfort.

"What's this I hear about another bidder?"

One step shy of the cement path leading to the cabana area, Nate pulled up short at his father's question. The last thing he wanted was his dad poking his greedy fingers into the deal, stirring the pot and making things difficult for Sofía.

Nate had told her they'd play fair. For that to happen, his father had to stay out of it.

"Nothing for you to worry about," Nate answered.

He purposefully kept his tone light, casual. His father had an uncanny knack for sensing any sign of weakness as if it were chum in the water. And like the shark Sofía had accused him of being, his dad would launch into attack mode.

Promise or no promise to his mom about keeping the family peace, Nate refused to let his father get at Sofía.

"What have you found out about them? Anything we

can use?"

Nate rubbed at the base of his neck and the ever-present tension headache his father's words exacerbated.

"It's early still," he hedged. "Might be a small group. I'm not sure about their ability to come up with the capital needed to convince the Land Planning Agency and city commission to lean their way. But they're motivated."

Not that Nate had any idea about the specific details of Sofía's bid. He *did* know she wasn't rolling in cash, and had to be working to piece together a suitable financial plan.

Then again, if there was anyone who could do the impossible, it was her. Strong, determined, savvy. Sofía's deep connection to Paradise Key and this resort would fuel her desire to win.

Those emotions could also be her downfall.

Not, however, if he had anything to do with it.

"Keep digging," his father ordered. "Everyone has a weak point. Find theirs. With land in that area scarce, this could be a nice piece to have for collateral or bargaining down the road. Now, how about the Sarasota site? How is that looking?"

Geez, Nate shook his head in amazement. Staring out at the open ocean, the midday sun glistening on its surface, he marveled at the ease with which his father switched from plotting the downfall of one competitor to setting his sights on another potential acquisition. That single-mindedness had increased the family fortunes Nate's grandfather had left them. It had also cost him relationships.

"I'm headed to Sarasota this weekend," Nate answered. "You'll have a full report next week. Probably—"

"Monday," his father interrupted. "I'll expect to see it by close of business."

Nate fumed, a curse word ready to roll off his tongue. Knowing his father would see anger as another weakness, Nate dialed back his initial retort and ground out, "You'll get the report when it's ready."

"Listen—"

"Dad, I'm doing my job down here. You looking over my shoulder is only going to hinder the process, and I know you have better things to do anyway. I've got this. Back off, okay?"

Several beats of tense silence ticked by.

Nate slid his gaze over the wildly overgrown grounds. Weed choked the flowerbeds, suffocating the buds struggling to bloom in the spring weather, like his father's demanding presence had always suffocated him.

"Get it done. You know what's expected of you."

Without waiting for a response, his father cut the line.

Disgusted, with his father for his superior attitude and with himself for putting up with it, Nate strode down the cement path until he reached the edge of the sandy beach.

Rather than remove his loafers for a walk, he hunkered down and scooped up a handful of sand. The tiny grains slipped through his fingers, leaving behind a dirty residue with bits that pricked his palm when he closed his fist. Much like his memories of Sofía and the life he'd once envisioned for himself, for them, pricked his heart.

As if it were yesterday, he recalled the purple and orange sunset sky. A hot, humidity-laden breeze teasing Sofía's silky hair. They'd spread a towel under the base of a palm tree, then sprawled on it side by side, wrapped in each other's arms, Sofía's long, tanned legs entwined with his. Her head on his chest, her spicy floral scent teasing him with each breath.

She had talked about her dream of working in the hotel and resort industry. Owning her own modest place, maybe a bed and breakfast in Miami, close to her parents.

He'd shared his secret desire. A hope, a burning need, to succeed in the family business, without turning into his father. And yet, he'd spent his adult life giving in to the man's edicts. Nearly marrying a woman he liked, but didn't love.

Walking away from the one woman he did.

Childish laughter drifted on the wind. Further down the beach, a group of kids had kicked off a game of two-on-two beach volleyball. A sad smile tugged the corners of Nate's mouth. There'd been a time when he and Sofía would have joined the fun. Called dibs on the next match.

Now they stood on opposite sides. Opponents on the resort's sand volleyball court whose existence was relegated to nothing more than a set of weather-roughened wooden poles standing apart, the net long disintegrated.

His dad would yell at him to spike the ball, win the point. Close out the match.

There had to be another way.

Could he win the bid for Hamilton, Inc., without devastating Sofía?

His father was the king of loopholes, side deals, and getting his way. From time to time, Nate had been told the apple didn't fall far from the tree in his family. Only, he planned to use the wily ways he'd learned from his father to see if there was some way, *any* way, to turn his predicament into a win-win situation.

Somehow, he'd keep his promises to his mom *and* Sofía. At the same time, if he were lucky, he'd find his way back into Sofía's good graces. Back into her arms and her life.

Rising to his feet, Nate headed up the walkway. Rather than make his way to lunch at the deli with Braddock as planned, he tapped out a quick message to let the commissioner know he'd have to take a rain check.

He was a man on a mission, with a winning game plan to devise.

"THANKS FOR HOSTING Evie, Lauren, and me Saturday night, Sal. I really appreciate your advice," Sofía told her mentor.

"Hell, it goes without saying you can count on me for anything. Vivian and I already talked it over, and we agree that you're a smart investment."

Seated at the dining room table in Tía Mili's condo late Monday morning, talking on the phone to Sal, Sofía's eyes misted at his words. The retired radio station owner from Jersey had been her mentor since she'd met him and his wife Vivian in Miami.

At the time, they'd been snowbirds living up North, but winter regulars at the boutique South Beach resort where Sofía was busy clawing her way up the ladder. In the six years since, Sal Bernardino had become her sounding board when politics and prejudice stood in her way. Sal and Vivi had played a huge role in her jump from hotel staff to manager when they asked her to take over running their three bed and breakfast homes in Key West.

Sofía owed them a lot. Which also meant she didn't want to take advantage of their goodwill.

"I appreciate you saying that, Sal. And I really appreciate your offer this past weekend."

"But you're not going to let me make this easier for you, are you?"

"No. That's not my style, and you know it."

"Hardheaded women, save me from them!" Sal's booming laughter was cut off by a short, hacking cough. Sofía heard what sounded like a few thumps to his burly chest before Sal spoke again. "Damn heartburn's been bugging me all morning."

"Make sure you take your meds," she reminded him.

"Yeah, yeah, Vivi nags me about that enough already."

"Good for her." Warmth for the couple spread through Sofía's chest. "It was wonderful to spend time with you and Vivi in St. Pete this weekend before you headed back to the Keys. I'm thrilled you were finally able to meet Lauren and Evie."

"Those two are powerhouses. Like you!" Sal's rumbling chuckle brought an answering smile to her face. "Vivi and I enjoyed seeing you three together. I'm sorry we never got the chance to know Lily."

"Me too, she was amazing." Regret tightened Sofía's chest in its painful grip. Lily's unexpected passing had stoked a fire within Sofía, heating her determination to a blue flame. "I'm sad her death is what brought the girls and me back here now. And yet, I wouldn't be making this move if I hadn't come home to honor her."

"If she was anything like the others, Lily would be proud of what you're doing," Sal assured her. "Hey, don't forget to give Jenna a hug from us. Tell her that we need to meet this new guy of hers, see if he gets my approval."

Sofía chuckled as Sal's tough-guy impersonation smoothed over the sentimental turn of their conversation. With his brawny build and thick Jersey accent, he did a convincing imitation of a wise guy who could put the screws to someone if needed. He was all talk, though, more prone to big bear hugs than fisticuffs.

On the other side of the counter separating the condo's open living, dining, kitchen area, Tía Mili paused in washing their breakfast dishes. Her brown eyes crinkled as she sent Sofía a smile of encouragement.

Dile hola, her tía mouthed. Sofía nodded.

"Tía Mili says hi, and I'll definitely pass along the message to Jenna," Sofía told Sal. "The girls and I are actually meeting at Scallywags later today." After her appointment with the bank's loan officer. Her stomach clenched with worry-tinged anticipation. "I better get going. Wanna make sure I've got everything squared away before this afternoon. You take care of yourself, big guy. Listen to Vivi and stop eating all that crap that makes you feel bad."

"It's all good. Just a little indigestion. Don't worry about me. You focus on what you gotta do there."

They exchanged good-byes, Sofía promising to update Sal and Vivi on how things went with the bank, then hung up.

"*Son buena gente, verdad?*" Tía Mili asked.

"*Sí*, they're good people. I was blessed to meet Vivi and Sal." Sofía smiled fondly, remembering that day. "Then to have them place their trust in me with their B&B's. They're *familia* now."

She set her phone next to a stack of the papers she'd spread out on the mottled cream, brown, and black marble veneer tabletop. "Sal gave me some good insight and advice after brunch yesterday while Vivi and the girls relaxed on the beach."

"The same way you took the time to guide me when I started my business." Tía Mili dried her hands on a blue kitchen towel as she skirted the counter to pull out a chair next to Sofía. "*El bien viene del bien.*"

Good comes from good. One of her tía's and her mami's favorite sayings. Handed down from their mami, Sofía's *abuela*, in Puerto Rico.

She sure hoped that was true. Because her Plan A—secure a larger loan in her name, with Sal and Vivi playing only a small investor role—was a long shot with the bank. The kind that had her texting Mami to ask for extra prayers.

Sofía drummed her fingers on the tabletop. She scanned the papers—financial statements, renovation plans, a scale drawing of her vision for the resort grounds and buildings, amongst others. Was this enough to convince the loan officer, a man who'd moved to Paradise Key a few years ago when his wife took a teaching position at the island's K-12 school? With no strong ties to the community and its residents, there'd be little chance of him giving Sofía any leeway as a local.

"You can do this, *nena*. I have faith in you." Tía Mili put her hand over Sofía's, gently silencing the nervous thrumming. "If you are determined, you will find a way. I know the resort is more than a piece of property to you. It holds precious memories, *no?*"

"Of course it does." Sofía twisted her hand to grasp her *tía's* tightly with her own. "It's what brought you and *tío* to Paradise Key. If that hadn't happened, I never would have met the girls."

"Or him."

Dios mío, Sofía's heart hiccupped, missing a few beats at Tía Mili's softly spoken words.

More than a godmother, her *madrina* had been a second mother to her. There for many of the big steps in Sofía's developing life.

She knew the only boy Sofía had dated in high school had been Nate. And while they'd kept their relationship quiet at the resort, there'd been no need to pretend at Tía Mili's house. *Familia* dinners. Date nights enjoying the sunset from the small dock near the condo. Movie nights on the couch, with Tía Mili watching or snoozing in her recliner nearby.

"Have you spoken with him again?"

"Again?" she asked, sidestepping the question. "How do you know I've spoken with him at all?"

Lame stall tactic. In a town as small as Paradise Key, with her tía's close connections, it's a wonder she hadn't known about Nate's arrival before Sofía had.

"The walk-through on Friday? Nathan was there, *verdad*?" Tía Mili raised her brows, an unspoken, "you can't fool me" in her wide-eyed expression.

"Right," Sofía confirmed.

Jenna's occasional complaints about everyone on the island knowing everyone else's business, whether she wanted them to or not, rang in Sofía's ears. Her lips twisted with a grimace. "I take it you ran into Vida at mass yesterday, huh?"

"*Sí.*"

"Then you know all there is to know. The Hamiltons plan to bid on the resort. I plan to beat them." And she would, if she could convince the bank to say yes.

The nervous anxiety she'd been struggling to quiet churned in her belly. Sofía pushed back her leather chair, its wooden legs scraping across the tile floor. Bending over the table, she gathered the papers, pushing down her laptop screen to slap it closed. Wishing it were that easy to close the unwanted direction this conversation had taken.

"You can't fool me, *sabes?*"

Sofía barely kept her eyes from rolling to the heavens. "Yes, I know."

"So talk to me. This cannot be easy for you. Nathan was your first love. Like my David."

"Oh no!" Sofía straightened with a jerk. She swatted a hand angrily through the air as if wiping away her *tía's* assertion. "It's not the same. What you had with Tío David was real. True love and commitment. Nate and me, that was fun times together, nothing more."

If she kept telling herself that lie, she'd eventually believe it. Then the pain of his decision to propose to Melanie, confirming Sofía's unspoken fear she'd never be considered good enough for the Hamilton name, would cease.

Tía Mili started to protest, but Sofía cut her off. "*Por favor*, let's not discuss it. Not now."

Face creased with worry, her *tía* plopped back in the leather dining chair.

"I have to concentrate on my pitch to the bank this afternoon," Sofía continued. "Without the loan, none of this—" she shook the papers in her hands, the desperation she'd hidden from her *familia* threatening to spew like lava, "—will matter."

"*Está bien*." Tía Mili nodded slowly, emphasizing her okay. "But remember, what is in here…" She tapped her temple with a finger. "It is not always the same as what lies here." She patted her chest, her brown eyes swimming with compassion. "And you are always wiser when you listen to them both."

Yes, that was probably true, Sofía mused as she finished packing everything into her computer bag. But when it came to Nate, her heart and her head had been at odds for years. One craving time with him, the other warning her away.

For her own sanity, she planned to heed that warning and keep her distance. Even if being in Paradise Key together made that more difficult.

Chapter Six

*A*S PRESENTED, IT'S *not a wise investment for the bank.*
Not a wise investment.

Sofía dragged her bare feet through the thick sand along Paradise Key beach, the dire words sounding a death knell in her head. Her conservative black heels, worn specifically for her appointment with the ultimately unyielding loan officer, dangled from two of her fingertips.

Despite her non-beach attire, she continued moving toward the water's edge. Dejection threatened. Frustration rode on its coattails, and she sought the calm she typically found amongst the sand, surf, and sun.

Gentle waves chased each other on and off the shore. The warm water and tiny sea-foam bubbles tickled the tops of her feet, washing against her ankles as the sand shifted below her.

"It *is* a wise investment," she grumbled. "*I'm* a wise investment."

She kicked the water in disgust. Then sucked her teeth with annoyance at the splash of droplets that flung back at her, leaving dark splotches on the skirt of her pale blue sheath dress.

It didn't matter. She was heading home for dinner with Tía Mili, so she could change before meeting the girls at Scallywags later. They'd all hoped it would be a celebratory night. Lauren, Evie, and Jenna had chimed in on their group text thread earlier, each wishing her good luck. They were almost as excited as Sofía about the potential for her to own the resort.

Fat chance of that happening. According to the straight-laced, no-special-consideration-for-locals-allowed loan officer.

The lazy surf rolled in and out from the Gulf, pulling the sand from beneath her feet. Sofía readjusted her stance and drew in a deep breath, willing her desperation to quiet. The briny smell of salt water and seaweed filled her lungs, the familiar scent working its magic. Like always.

A morning run along the shore, a walk before sunset. Hanging out under the boardwalk's shade in the heat of the day. It didn't matter—the beach never failed to energize and reset her psyche.

Eyes closed, she raised her face to the sun. The heat in-fused her, and she imagined its energy squashing the negativity threatening to overcome her confidence.

"Everything okay?" a deep voice asked from behind her.

Sofía started, spinning around so fast one of her heels slipped off her fingertips. She made a grab for it, but the shoe bounced off the palm of her free hand and flew through the air.

"Whoa!" Nate snagged it midair, his eyes widening in surprise. "Can't say I've ever had a woman throw her shoe at me in hello. Good-bye, well, maybe once or twice."

He flashed his sexy grin, looking all relaxed and carefree in a short-sleeved, soft green and white checkered Oxford and khaki cargo shorts. His light brown hair was mussed from the wind, and he'd obviously been out in the sun over the weekend based on his newly acquired golden tan.

For some perverse reason, the idea he'd been idly lazing around at the beach the past few days had her frustration mushrooming again.

"What are you doing here?" she complained. Forget the fact that his quick reflexes had saved her favorite pair of business heels from a sure ruin.

"Nice to see you, too. It's a public beach," he added when she frowned at his initial answer. "Everyone's welcome."

She held out her hand for her shoe.

Nate ignored her, turning it over in his hands, studying it as if he'd never seen a sensible black leather pump before.

Sofía barely held back a sigh. The closeness they'd once shared, that she still pined for in the tiniest corner of her heart, alerted her to what was coming.

Sure enough, Nate angled his head to slant an inquisitive look at her. The one that said he knew something was bugging her, and he didn't plan on backing down until she spilled her guts.

There'd been a time when that beguiling expression on his handsome face, the expectant flash in his green eyes, would have cajoled her into confiding in him. He was, despite his good-time-guy persona, a smart sounding board. Between Nate and Sal, she'd benefitted from their keen advice over the years.

Things were different now, though.

Had been from the moment Nate had mentioned his father's demand that Nate propose to Melanie. Or rather, when Nate hadn't immediately said no, she'd realized the true strength of his family's pull. All those times she had encouraged him to fight for his rightful place, for the dream he had of overseeing his own small group of resorts under the Hamilton name. Within the company, yet apart from his father. In the defining moment, they hadn't mattered.

He'd flown to Key West to tell her in person, but she hadn't offered any input on his decision. She couldn't.

Secretly, she'd been hoping he'd make the right choice on his own. When the news of his engagement had been released the next week, her faith in his ability to break away from his father's influence had cracked. Shattering her heart along with it.

Now, as much as it pained her, she couldn't trust that if she shared her loan problem with Nate, it wouldn't get back to his father, who'd most certainly use the information to cripple her chances at winning the bid.

A seagull squawked as it glided over their heads, its grey

wings spread wide. The little bird dipped, then swooped to land a few feet away. It stutter-stepped along the sand, stopping to peck its beak at the little piles of sea grass strung along the shore. Just like Nate's charming personality could peck away at her resolve to not give into the part of her that ached to be with him again.

She had to silence the cry. If not, it could only lead to inevitable heartbreak. Again.

He waited, patient, not pushing, but not going away either.

One of the things that drew her to him was his propensity to take care of those closest to him. Nate would bend over backward to help them. He had an uncanny knack for showing up when she least expected, but needed it the most. There to magically turn a crappy day into a magical weekend.

"Interesting shoe choice for a walk on the beach," he mused. His large hands fondled her heel, caressing the black leather. "Unless this unplanned visit is more along the lines of one of those head-clearing visits you're fond of."

She knew this routine. If she stayed quiet and didn't engage, he'd simply continue talking to himself. Waiting her out.

"Hello, Nathan," Sofía answered, working to keep her voice bland. "It's lovely to see you. Unfortunately, I was just leaving. May I please have my shoe?"

"Will you walk with me?" He tilted his head invitingly,

his expression hopeful.

¡Sí! her heart cried.

¡No! ¿Estás loca? her brain answered.

Of course she'd be crazy to say yes. Or a glutton for punishment. Neither option was good.

After a beat, Nate took a hesitant step in the direction that would eventually lead to Tía Mili's house. That was the only reason she followed him, because she was headed that way anyway. At least, it was what she told herself.

"What's going on?" he asked.

"Nothing."

He moved to her left side, keeping his sneakers out of reach of the tide's ever-moving fingers. "That's all you're gonna say?"

"Yep."

His husky chuckle brushed against her soul, sending tingles of desire rippling through her. Doggedly, she ignored them.

She waded deeper into the rolling surf, confident he wouldn't follow. A wave flooded in, splashing up her calves, and she tugged her dress hem above her knees.

"I know you, Sof." Nate glanced at her, nostalgia and concern shadowing his eyes before he glanced away. "Whether it's that little V in between your brows. The way you drag your hand through your hair, gripping the ends in your fist. Or how you head to the water to refill your well. They're your tells. At least, for me they are."

Coño, he had her pegged. And double damn his words for arrowing straight to her heart.

"We're on opposite sides here, Nate." She laid the truth out there to remind herself as much as him. "There's no way I'm feeding Hamilton, Inc., insider info."

He drew to an abrupt stop, either not caring or not noticing the inches-high wave that covered the toes of his pricey sneakers.

Sofía slowed her steps, turning to squint back at him.

"Forget Hamilton, Inc. Forget my father. Don't think about anything or anyone else." He flung out an arm as if to encompass the world around them. Then, like the motion had taken the wind out of his parasail, he dropped his arm at his side. "It's just us here. Talk to me. Let me help you. Please."

He clasped his hands together on the last word.

The juxtaposition of her black heel pressed against his muscular chest should have been comical. But the honest sincerity blanketing his chiseled features, the plea in his sea-green eyes, called to her.

This was her Nate.

The guy who randomly sent her silly texts to make her laugh.

Who special ordered her a bottle of Don Q rather than flowers, so they could video chat and "have a drink together."

Who'd hopped a last-minute flight to Key West so he

could give her a hug because he'd heard the deep pain in her voice when he'd called to check on her after her *abuela's* funeral.

And if she were honest with herself, the first person she'd thought to call when she'd found out about Lily's death.

Ay, her heart swelled, overwhelmed by the need to be able to trust him again. Sofía gripped the shoulder strap on her tote bag, torn between what her head and her heart urged her to do.

Her gaze slid past Nate's shoulder to the resort looming behind him. It had once been their Shangri-La. Tía Mili was right, even if Sofía refused to admit it out loud.

Part of why she wanted the resort so badly was because of the important role it had played in shaping her life. Nate was irrevocably tied to that. If they couldn't be together, at least she'd see this part of their memory flourish. It would be both a personal and professional win.

Only, right now, that win was in jeopardy.

Sal would tell her to quit over-thinking it and take him up on his Plan-B offer. Nate—*her* Nate—could provide an unbiased perspective.

Heaving a soul-weary sigh, she went for broke. "The bank's loan officer turned down my application."

Nate's eyes widened a fraction, then he quickly grew serious. "Does the Local Planning Agency know? You want to keep that under wraps until you can figure out other financing."

"I haven't shared the news with anyone else. But in this town, who knows how long I have before word gets out."

Nate nodded, then started walking again. She fell into step beside him, remembering his habit of pacing while the wheels in his head were turning.

"Okay, so I'm assuming you have a few other options in your back pocket, right?"

"Uh-huh." She drew out the word.

Nate must have sensed her hesitancy because he glanced over at her at the same time he sidestepped a rush of sea-foam-coated water.

"I have a backer, someone who will give me the money flat out. Under our own terms."

"But?"

"But I'm not sure I want to go that route. I want this on my own."

"And somehow taking Sal's offer means you're not doing that?"

Sofía narrowed her eyes at Nate, annoyed by his keen perception.

"Why would I not guess it's him?" Nate's shoulders lifted and dropped in a "Duh!" shrug. "The guy's like a father to you. How many times have you told me Sal and Vivi are *familia*? Believe me, I understand how much your *familia*, in all its forms, means to you."

Disappointment burned in Sofía's chest. Not too long ago, Nate had been included in that group.

"Here's the thing." Nate grasped her elbow, drawing her to a stop. Warmth seeped up her arm at his touch. "As much as they say, 'it's business, not personal,' that's not always the truth. Trust *is* personal. And when you go into business with someone, you've gotta be able to trust them."

His hand slid from her elbow up her arm to cup her shoulder. Sofía grabbed onto her tote bag straps, desperately fighting the urge to place her hands at his waist and lean into his embrace.

"When it comes to business, there's no one you trust more than Sal, right?"

He gazed down at her intently. His expression serious.

Somehow, she felt like this was a trick question. Confused, uncertain why that would be true, she nodded.

Nate let out a little huff of breath, his mouth grim. He stepped back, breaking their connection. "Then you have to ask yourself—is your pride in wanting your name to be the one listed as main investor on the loan more important than partnering with someone you have one hundred percent confidence in?"

Without another word, he turned to start walking again. They neared the part of the beach that curved to the northeast side of the island. Out of habit for her, and probably based on memory for him, they made their way up the dry sand to the walkway leading from the beach to Old Mill Drive and Tía Mili's condo.

When they reached the sidewalk, Nate held out her black

heel. "You deserve to win this, Sof. Others might try to make it difficult for you, but don't let pride stop you from getting what you want. What we both know you've worked hard for."

He leaned down to brush a kiss along her left cheek. "Give Tía Mili my best. See you around."

Before she could recover from her surprise—at both his words of encouragement and the rush of desire that suffused her body the instant his lips touched her skin—Nate strode away.

A lump of mixed emotions clogging her throat, Sofía watched him go.

He was dangerous that one. Dangerous to her heart and her peace of mind. She'd do well to remember that and keep her distance.

"YOU WANT ANOTHER, or are you good?"

Nate glanced up from staring into his nearly empty whiskey glass to find Delilah Firth a few feet away from his stool.

The young single mom who worked behind the bar at Scallywags popped the caps off two beer bottles with an easy flick of her wrist. She set the drinks at the end of the bar for a waitress, going about her business without trying to up-sell him anything.

He liked the redhead's style. Her friendly eyes and quick smile led to easy conversation when he was in the mood to talk, but she had a good feel for when her patrons were here for the drinks and not idle chatter. Like him, tonight.

"I'm good, thanks," he answered.

Delilah jutted her chin in acknowledgement, then pulled the tap handle with a local Gainesville brewery's logo to fill a pint glass.

Across the bar, a throaty laugh drew his attention. He couldn't ignore Sofía's presence even if he tried.

She and the rest of the girls sat at their regular table. Talking, eating, comfortable with each other in a way that spoke of shared experiences. It was almost like back in the day when he'd catch up to them gathered at Delightful Scoops or Deli 2389. Only, Lily was missing. An empty chair amongst them.

The other night, it'd been filled by the surfer-looking guy who had come with Jenna. Tonight, she'd arrived alone, although she'd spent most of the evening eyeing the door.

Empty appetizer plates and utensils along with glasses that had once held water, soda, or bar drinks littered their table's surface. Lauren said something Nate couldn't hear, and Sofía's full lips curved. The smile crinkled the corners of her hazel eyes. Head tilted to the side, Sofía's hair draped down her arm and along the curve of her breast in a silky black curtain.

Damn, she was so beautiful it made his heart ache. She

looked relaxed, the distress he'd seen earlier on the beach dissipated thanks to her friends. As much as he wanted to do that for her, it was good to know the girls were there.

Nate drained the last sip of his whiskey. The liquid burned a trail down his throat, seeping into his chest. Just like the slow burn he had always carried for Sofía.

Walking along the water with her today had given him a bittersweet taste of what they'd once shared. Starting when they'd been young and carefree, and continuing into their adult lives.

Their conversation had always been easy. Sure, they side-stepped a topic or two, namely his dad's unyielding expectations. Nate had done his best to always be an honest opinion she could rely on, especially when it came to business advice. She had occasionally challenged him to act on his idea to create a boutique hotel division within Hamilton, Inc. Since their breakup, he'd gone full steam ahead with it, only to be hit with roadblock after roadblock by his father.

For years, Nate had towed the line when it came to family business. Making waves outside the office where his father rarely paid him any attention. Until the old man had handed down his "propose to Melanie" edict.

Recalling that whole fiasco nearly had Nate signaling for another whiskey. Ashamed about how he'd allowed his mother to convince him the arrangement was for the best. In the secret part of his soul, he admitted to himself that he had wanted Sofía to tell him not to do it. Hoped she would have given him some kind of sign, encouraging him to fight for them.

But she hadn't.

She pushed him away with that damn "no-strings-attached" promise.

Foolishly, he and Melanie had gone along with the engagement. Pretending it would be okay. Tip-toeing around the truth they read in the other's eyes. Wanting to cry foul and call the whole thing off.

Nate should have. But after Sofía had severed ties, he dove into researching boutique properties, almost frantic to see the only other thing he'd wanted come to fruition.

Thankfully, Melanie had seen the light. Or rather, the bright lights of Vegas where she'd run off for a quickie wedding with the artist she'd secretly fallen in love with several years ago. Much to her parents' disappointment.

And he...he was here, back in Paradise Key, the place that had given him his first real taste of home. Of *familia* as Sofía said. For him, hearing the word *family* in Spanish made it come to life. Made the possibility real. He wanted that.

"It's okay. I'm leaving right behind you. Go on." Sofía's voice drew Nate's attention.

He glanced up to find her standing in the entry. She hugged Jenna, Lauren, and Evie good-bye, then headed into the ladies' room.

Nate saluted Evie with his empty glass when she gave him a half-hearted wave. Earlier, when she'd swung by his stool to say hello, she'd made it clear Hamilton, Inc. had no business bidding on the resort. Little did she know, he was banking on that fact.

His weekend trip to Sarasota had provided some valuable details that could back up his recommendation the company drop its interest in the resort here and focus efforts on the larger property down south. His call this morning had set a few other pieces in motion that should help solidify his plan.

Numbers were key when it came to Nathan Hamilton, II. All he cared about was the bottom-line financial gain. Nate planned to give him that proof.

The door to the ladies' room opened, emitting the faint trill of salsa music. Sofía's ringtone on her cell.

She stepped out, pausing near the hostess stand to pull her phone out of her back jeans pocket. Nate read the hello on her smiling lips as she answered. Seconds later, shock registered on her face and she sank onto one of the wooden chairs lined up against the wall.

Her tanned skin turned a pasty cream color as she covered her mouth with a hand Nate could have sworn trembled. In a flash, he was off his stool and at her side.

"A heart attack? Is he-is he conscious?" Her voice shook on the stuttered question.

Nate couldn't hear what was said on the other end, but based on Sofía's pain-filled gasp, it couldn't have been good news.

"Oh, Vivi, that must have been so scary for you," Sofía

murmured.

Nate's stomach clenched when he heard who she was speaking with. Vivi had to be calling about Sal. For the older woman's sake, and especially for Sofía's, since she just buried one of her best friends, he hoped the older man was fighting to survive.

"Have you talked to your boys? Are they coming?"

Nate could hear Vivi's voice through the phone, but he wasn't able to make out her response.

"I see. *Ay Dios*, I'm so sorry I'm not there with you. Give me…" Sofía broke off. Her gaze flitted around the open bar area as if searching for something. "I don't know how long it'll take me, but I'm coming down."

She clenched her fist on her lap, practically vibrating with the intensity of her emotions. Nate covered her hand with his own.

The worry for her building in his chest eased the slightest bit when she twisted her wrist and uncurled her fingers to link them with his. She shot him a look filled with so much pain and fear it took his breath away.

"I'll be there tomorrow, Vivi," Sofía promised. "As early as I can. You be strong, okay?"

She worried her lower lip, shaking her head as she listened to Vivi's response.

"I can work on the bid from Key West as well as I can from here. You don't need to be there alone."

Nate sat quietly while Sofía finished her conversation. It

mostly consisted of her reassuring Vivi that she could count on Sofía to be at her side tomorrow come hell or high water. And that she'd ask her mom and Tía Mili to add Sal to their prayer chains.

Eventually, Sofía hung up. As soon as she did, her torso curled in on itself as if someone had punched her in the stomach. She collapsed with her elbows on her thighs, burying her face in her palms.

Nate gently stroked her back, desperate to offer some reassurance. She heaved several shuddering breaths, but didn't say anything.

The main door to the bar opened, and a rowdy group of college coeds entered. Voices loud, they joked about some prank one or the other had pulled.

"I've gotta get out of here." Sofía pushed herself to a stand, slinging the strap of the same dark brown tote she'd carried at the beach over her shoulder.

"Let's go."

One hand on the small of her back, the other motioning for the coeds to make room for them to pass by, Nate ushered her toward the door.

Out on the boardwalk, the quiet of early evening greeted them. The sun had set, leaving the sky a dark navy blue speckled with twinkling stars. Out on the water, the occasional buoy light flickered a hello to those on land.

Sofía strode down the planked walkway in the direction of her home. The soft breeze blew her hair, and she tossed her head to get the tresses out of her face.

"What's your plan?" he asked.

Her brows furrowed, creating a little V between them. In another place and time, he would have pulled her gently to his side to kiss the worry spot. Now all he could do was wait to see what she had in mind, so he could figure out how best to help her.

"I'm sure by the time I made it down to Tampa tonight, I'd miss the last flight to Key West. If I haven't already." She huffed out a frustrated breath. "If I wait until morning to fly down, by the time I get there it could be too late...*ay Dios, por favor, no...*"

Her voice trailed off and she pulled to a stop, stumbling several paces until she leaned against the wooden railing overlooking the darkened ocean. The nearby streetlamp cast its hue over them, leaving her face a mix of shadow and light. She wove her fingers through her hair, grabbing the strands in a tight grip. Her "I'm beyond frustrated" tell.

"Let's drive," he suggested.

"I don't have a car. Evie and I landed around the same time, so I rode up with her."

"No, I mean, let *me* drive you," he clarified. "I've got a rental."

She craned her neck to shoot him her typical "*estás loco*" glare.

Yes, he was crazy. Crazy about her. Crazy serious about doing whatever he could to show her how much he cared. Because even if she no longer returned his feelings, he'd do anything for her.

He joined her at the railing, resting his elbows on the wooden plank. His shoulder brushed hers, but he purposefully stayed glued to her side. A sign he wasn't going anywhere.

"It's late. You're upset. Who the hell wouldn't be in your position? I have a car and time to spare." Determined to convince her, yet knowing better than to push, he stared out at the gently lapping water, calmly cataloguing the reasons why his idea was a solid one. "Plus, it's an eight-hour drive down the Keys, and we both know it can get monotonous. That's not the best thing to undertake on your own this late at night. You've told me that before, right?"

When she didn't respond, Nate glanced at Sofía to find her gaping at him. Her puzzled frown told him she was struggling to come up with a way to refute his points. He knew she couldn't, but he didn't want to give her time to think of something anyway.

"Sof, please." He straightened, angling his body to face her. When she did the same, he grasped her upper arms, his hold light but certain. "Let me do this for you. Let me help you."

"Why?" she asked, her voice a raspy whisper.

"Because…" He faltered.

He couldn't admit he wanted her back. Not yet. If he said the words too soon, she'd put up those walls between them she was so freaking expert at erecting. He had to take this slow. *Show* her he was serious.

"Because it's what friends do for each other. Because I know you'd do it for me, if the situation was reversed."

She eyed him silently for several heart-pounding seconds, her expression serious. Then she reached out to hook a finger in between two of the buttons on his Oxford, surprising him by leaning forward to rest her forehead on the front of his right shoulder.

Her spicy floral scent filled his lungs on his next breath. He held it, her essence coursing through his blood like a potent stimulant.

When she eventually tilted her head to peer up at him, tears shone in her beautiful eyes. She stepped closer, her sandaled feet nearly touching his Sperrys.

"You don't make this easy, *sabes?*"

"No, I don't know," he answered truthfully. "I think it's a pretty easy decision. I mean, why would you turn down a chauffeured trip, huh?"

She offered him a watery smile. Then, as if in slow motion, she rose onto her toes to brush her lips over his. Her hands gripped his shirt at his waist, and it was only natural for him to wrap her in his arms.

Home. She felt like home. And he like a traveler too long on the road.

The soft touch of her lips had his body urging him to deepen the kiss, to remind her of the amazing passion they'd always shared.

His head, even his wounded heart, warned him to take it slow.

Sofía lowered from her tiptoes, but stayed in the circle of his embrace. She licked her lips as if savoring his taste.

Nate nearly groaned out loud. He pressed his forehead to hers, willing his body to cool and his pulse to slow.

"Okay," Sofía murmured. "I accept your offer."

Yes!

The word shot through his brain like one of the fireworks they used to watch launching over the water during the town's July 4th celebration.

Rather than pump his fist in triumph like he wanted, Nate cupped her cheeks, then dropped a soft kiss onto her nose.

Her lips curved in the hint of a smile that thankfully reached her tear-filled eyes.

"Gracias," she whispered.

"Anytime."

Her eyes drifted close, and, because he couldn't *not* do it, Nate covered her lips with his, softly nipping at her sweetness. Sofía leaned into his kiss, and his pulse sparked. He craved more, but while her response gave him confidence, he knew now wasn't the right time. She needed to get to her *familia*. He could give her that. And he'd gladly do so.

Easing back, away from her temptation, he reached for her hands.

"Come on," he told her, linking their fingers together. "Let's get you to Sal and Vivi."

Chapter Seven

S OFÍA CAME AWAKE with a start. For a second, she didn't remember where she was and she panicked, sitting bolt upright. Her seat belt engaged, jerking her to an abrupt stop.

"Hey, sleepy head," Nate teased from the driver's seat beside her.

In an instant, the events from last night—Vivi's terrible call, Nate's offer to drive her down, the awkwardness of asking him to wait outside of Tía Mili's house when he arrived to pick her up, but not admitting it was because she wanted to avoid the twenty questions her *tía* would certainly ask…everything rushed back on her like a tidal wave.

Fear for Sal slewed through her. It swirled into an unpleasant mix along with her discomfort over relying on Nate and her determination to keep her guard up around him.

"Hi," she said, massaging the crick in her neck.

Nate took his gaze off the road briefly to shoot her a lazy grin that belied the lines of fatigue fanning out from the corners of his eyes. The rising sun painted the horizon behind him in a mix of deep orange and rich peach hues. Tired shadows darkened the skin under his eyes, matching the shadowed clouds in the sky with the early morning rays peeking out from behind them.

"Are we already at the Seven Mile Bridge?" She scrubbed her hands over her face, thinking she must still be groggy. No way had she been asleep that long.

"Yep," Nate answered.

Sure enough, a quick glance at the open ocean spread out to the right and left of the car and the long stretch of road ahead of them confirmed they'd already reached the well-known bridge just south of Marathon Key.

"*Dios mío*, when did I nod off?"

"Right after we passed Port St. Lucie." Nate tipped a paper coffee cup with a gas station logo to his lips.

Surprised, Sofía realized he must have stopped for the pick-me-up caffeine without her even waking up.

"I can't believe I slept over four hours. So much for helping you drive. We're only about forty-five minutes out." She tucked a loose strand of hair back into her ponytail, then twisted around to face Nate.

"You needed the rest." His left elbow propped on his windowsill, Nate took another sip of coffee. "Worrying the whole trip down wouldn't have helped you. Or Vivi and Sal. But your phone has been blowing up for the past thirty minutes or so. Mili and your mom are definitely early risers. You might wanna give them a call."

He glanced down at her cell, resting in the console between the two front seats.

"Or I can pull over and stretch my legs so you can talk to

them in private if you'd prefer," he added.

It was the first time he had acknowledged her strange behavior last night. On his way to pick her up, he'd mentioned it would be good to see Tía Mili again. Sofía had quickly shut him down, telling him there was no need for him to come inside. Something her *tía* had been adamant he do when Sofía and Nate had hung out together as teens.

"*Un novio debe tocar la puerta y decirle hola a tu familia antes de sacarte para pasear.*"

True, a boyfriend should knock on the door and greet a girl's family before they went out on a date. But Nate hadn't been her boyfriend for a long time now, and this was most definitely *not* a date. He was a friend, kind of, helping her in a jam.

Instead, she had raced down the outside stairs to the parking area where he waited. Nate had taken her overnight bag to stow in the trunk of his rental car without saying a word. Then, after ensuring she was ready to go, he'd turned his convertible off Mill Drive onto 2nd Street, heading toward Highway 24, which would take them off the island.

For the first three and a half hours of their drive, before she'd gone Rip Van Winkle on him, conversation was minimal. She'd been struggling to remain calm while inside she was stressing over Sal's health and worrying about Vivi being on her own since both their sons lived up North and were out of the country on business. It helped that the Bernardino B&Bs were in the capable hands of Paul, Sofía's assistant manager. While prone to exaggeration and sharing his sometimes-inappropriate opinions, the middle-aged man had years of bed and breakfast experience and a good feel for how she preferred the show to run.

Between calls with Paul, her texts to Lauren, Jenna, and Evie letting them know she'd had to leave Paradise Key suddenly and why, along with messages to her *mami* and Vivi alerting them that she was on the road—which had set of a firestorm of responses from all the women—Sofía had been glued to her cell those first couple of hours of the drive.

Nate had taken her cue and stayed mum. Eventually, with his phone synched to the car's stereo, he had adjusted the volume so Ed Sheeran's melodious voice serenaded them softly. A subtle reminder, for her at least, of the time she'd been in Manhattan for a conference and Nate had surprised her with Ed Sheeran concert tickets.

It was probably why she'd fallen asleep once her phone had quieted. Avoiding the memories, unwilling to relive them with him, she'd rested her head against her side window. And promptly dozed off.

Now Sofía picked up her cell to scroll through the messages and missed call alerts. *Dios mío*, Nate was right. Two calls from her mom. One from her *tía*. Multiple texts from each.

"Want me to pull over when we get to Bahia Honda?" Nate asked.

The state park entrance area would be a good place for

him to walk around, but she was anxious to get to the Lower Keys Medical Center. "That's okay. I'll call when we get to the hospital and have an update."

"Do your mom and Mili know you're with me?"

It was a simple question, but with multiple responses. The deeper answer was loaded down by the years of her and Nate's shared history and double the maternal concern. Sofía opted for the lighter, equally as true answer instead. "You think Tía Mili would let me get in a car without her knowing who was behind the wheel? Even at my age?"

Nate huffed out a laugh. "Point made."

His expression sobered. The muscle in his jaw tightened as if he struggled with something. When he finally spoke again, his voice was gruff with unease. "Whatever else has happened between us, Sof, or whatever you've shared with your mom and Mili, I guess, I hope they both know they can count on me to keep you safe."

"They do." She did too, physically.

Emotionally? There was no need for him to know Mami and Tía Mili held fast to the opinion that Sofía had never maintained a long-term relationship with another man because of Nate. Tía Mili had spent more time with him when they were younger, so she had a soft spot for Nate. Mami and Papi had met him twice when Nate had visited Miami after college. None of them knew about the weekend visits and occasional dalliances over the years. And yet, her mom and *tía* maintained their stance.

Frankly, their theory on why she had yet to marry and pop out a grandbaby they could spoil was not something she chose to think about. Much less share with him.

"That's good to know." Nate said the words on a tired sigh as he rubbed the sleep from his eyes with the back of his left hand.

"Want me to take over for the last little bit?" she asked.

"Naw, I'm good. I'll sleep after I drop you off at the hospital and figure out where I'm going to stay."

Guilt pinched her belly. He'd dropped everything to make this trip with her. She hadn't even asked about his work schedule or if his father expected him to be somewhere else. Nate was going out of his way for her. The least she could do was put him up for the night, before he left tomorrow.

"If you haven't booked anything, you can stay at my place. If you want," she offered.

Nate's double take was classic sitcom quality. He twisted in his seat, angling his torso toward her as his gaze continued alternating between her and the road ahead. His green eyes flashed both question and surprise.

"Are you sure?"

Not really, the voice of reason whispered in her head. Stubbornly, she silenced it. "Yes."

His shoulders visibly relaxed.

"I'd like that." The warm smile he gave her before focusing back on the road had her insides melting.

Stop it, she chided herself. This was merely a thank you for his help. And only for one night.

What could it possibly hurt?

"PAUL, SERIOUSLY," NATE told the assistant manager at Bernardino's B&B. "If you want to touch base with the kitchen staff to make sure everything is running smoothly for breakfast, I don't mind covering the front desk and answering any questions for guests who stop by."

They stood near the Art Deco-painted wooden secretary desk in the living room at the largest of the three bed and breakfast homes Sal and Vivi owned in Key West.

"Oh no, I couldn't possibly ask you to do that." A tall, lanky older guy, Paul waved off Nate's offer with his manicured left hand. His silver wedding band and a black and silver thumb ring caught the sunlight streaming in through the windows lining the front wall of the three-story Victorian home. A rainbow-colored mix of leather strap bracelets adorned his wrist, matching the miniature rainbows splashed across his short-sleeved button-down. "Sofía called to say you'd be heading to her bungalow in the back of the property. I can show you the way. Come on, honey."

Spinning on his loafered heel, Paul sashayed through the B&B's first floor, passed the kitchen, and out the back door. They stepped onto a wooden deck with an amoeba-shaped jacuzzi nestled center stage. The backyard teemed with thick vegetation blooming with late spring flowers. Bright orange and purple plumed Birds of Paradise fought for attention amid red and white bleeding hearts, pink and yellow hibiscus, and deep purple orchids. Bougainvillea vines climbed the privacy fence, their bright pink and fuchsia petals creating a backdrop of vibrant colors.

In the far right corner of the oversized lot, a large banyan tree held court, limbs arching through the air to provide shade for those seeking relaxation. The tree's aerial roots stretched down from the limbs to the ground below, enveloping the trunk in a visual masterpiece of nature.

To the left of the banyan tree, at the property's far edge, sat Sofía's bungalow. Once a private suite for guests, Sal and Vivi had turned the brightly painted studio apartment over to Sofía as part of the enticement package when they'd lured her away from Miami.

Nate followed Paul up the four steps leading to the raised porch that ran the length of the small building, the height a necessary hurricane flood water precaution. The soft pink exterior with white trim matched the main house's Victorian design. An aloe plant and an orchid nestled in clay pots greeted him, along with a "*Bienvenidos*" jute mat in front of the red painted door.

"Home sweet home," Paul sing-songed. He unlocked the deadbolt, then handed the spare key to Nate with a flourish. "If there's anything you need, don't hesitate. It's a little crazy around here at the moment. With Sofía at the funeral and now Sal scaring ten years off all our lives…well, I'm hobbling around like a dame with one stiletto heel snapped off." He pressed a palm to his chest, giving an exaggerated sigh. "But it's all good. Praise whomever or whatever floats your boat, as long as Sal's back to his lovable gruff self soon enough, we'll all be fine."

As much as Nate wanted a shower followed by uninterrupted shuteye, if there was one thing he could handle while half asleep, it was running a small operation like Bernardino's. Even if there were two other smaller properties in the mix. He knew Sal and Vivi had stepped up to carry a little extra weight around here when Sofía had raced off to Paradise Key for Lily's services. Without the older couple for back up, Paul had to be juggling quite a bit.

"Look, why don't I get cleaned up, and then, as long as you can keep pouring me fresh coffee, I'm an extra pair of hands for whatever you need during the morning rush." Nate understood the importance of welcoming guests to the free full breakfast, ensuring their day started off with a friendly face before they either ventured out to tour the island or checked out knowing their stay was appreciated. While guests were being attended, other staff stayed busy handling the day-to-day tasks behind the scenes that kept the properties running smoothly. Chipping in to help was easily something he could do to alleviate some of the stress on Sofía.

Paul tucked his chin, his assessing gaze combing Nate from head to Sperrys and back up again. "Are you offering your services?"

Paul's arched brow punctuated his innuendo, and Nate threw back his head on a laugh.

"As a breakfast chafing dish replenisher, front desk direction giver, bed linen changer…I'm your guy."

"Pity, I got all excited for a second there." Paul's teasing wink assured Nate they were going to get along just fine. Which was good, because he planned to stay here as long as Sofía needed him.

"Let me grab a shower and quick change. I'll head over to the main house shortly." Nate twisted the knob, then pushed the door open. Behind him, he heard Paul clamber down the wooden stairs.

"Oh, and one more thing."

Paul's call had Nate turning around to see what the assistant manager might need.

"Sofía's pretty hush-hush about her private life. But that doesn't mean I won't do a little prying." Brown eyes flashing with a playful warning, Paul waggled a finger at Nate. "She's a gem, that one. Not all are worthy of her."

On that note, Paul strutted away, thin hips shaking side to side in his pale blue linen walking shorts.

Nate didn't have to be reminded of Sofía's worth. He'd known it all along. Stupidly, he'd held back in the past, wanting her to voice her opinion on where they stood, rather than him revealing his feelings for her first. Too afraid of rejection.

Yet, it was what he'd ended up with anyway.

Sofía cutting all ties had gutted him. Melanie being strong enough to stand up to her family had put him in a tailspin of self-approach that, for a brief period, had landed him at the bottom of a whiskey bottle. Or two or three.

This second banishment to Paradise Key had been like an antibiotic shot in the arm, starting him on the road to recovery. Though not down the path his father anticipated.

No, Nate had an idea for a new plan with a different end goal. It wasn't going to be easy. He'd have to finesse some conversations, dig deeper into his research, crunch a lot of numbers, and hope his assessments were correct. The final step would involve convincing several key people.

At the top of his list: Sofía.

Chapter Eight

S OFÍA STARTED TO take the stone-marked walkway leading from the front yard at Bernardino's along the left side of the main house around to the back. It was the closest, fastest route to a warm shower and comfy bed. She had just enough time for a thirty-minute power nap before she picked up Vivian and headed back to the hospital in a couple of hours.

Instead, she veered toward the steps leading up to the wide verandah that wrapped the perimeter of the first floor. It was already two in the afternoon, nearly check-in time. Despite her fatigue, she should make sure Paul had been able to keep everything on track. Especially since every room at Bernardino's was booked.

Out of habit, she scanned the open verandah, making sure no cobwebs hung from the white gingerbread trim adorning the framework. The aloe plants and orchids had been watered, their pots strategically placed around the two blue and sea-foam green rockers nestled on opposite sides of a white-framed ceramic tile-topped end table. It was a comfy spot to people watch or enjoy the cooler spring weather in the early mornings or late evenings.

The urge to sink into one of the rockers and let the gentle swaying lull her to sleep, bringing her a respite from the running worry-filled commentary in her head, was tempting. The past twenty-four hours had dealt her two serious blows. First the bank's denial, then Sal's heart attack. But responsibilities awaited her inside. Poor Paul had been left to handle all three locations on his own today, with two employees having called out sick.

Wearily, Sofía pushed open the front door. The sound of classical music playing softly in the background greeted her. Paul's favorite mood relaxing station. Unfortunately, the music's tranquil vibe was shattered by his screech of surprise when he saw her.

Before she could react, her assistant manager raced around the check-in desk along the far right wall in the family room. As soon as he reached her, Paul threw his scrawny arms around her in a pretty good rendition of a bone-crunching bear hug.

"Good God, it is such a relief to see you! How's the big guy doing? I know he's out of surgery, but what are his doctors saying? When are we going to have him back here driving me crazy? How's Vivi? I can't imagine what that poor woman is going through? And you!"

Paul finally pulled back from his death-squeeze hug, only to grab onto Sofía's shoulders and give her a little shake. "What's with you holding out on me when it comes to this new *manfriend* of yours?"

The mix of emotions in Paul's voice, racing from concern to despair to scandalized accusation, had Sofía's head spinning. Whether from lack of good sleep, her hyperstressed state, or her disillusion over the increasing odds of her being able to win the Paradise Key Resort bid, she had a hard time following his rapid-fire questions.

"Honey, where have you been hiding him? He is a hunk with a capital H!" Paul's sotto-voce impersonation didn't quite work when he tacked on a loud, lip-smacking, "Mm-mm!"

On cue, Nate strolled out of the laundry room at the end of the main floor hallway. His arm muscles flexed beneath his T-shirt sleeves as he hefted a plastic basket filled with folded white beach towels in front of him. Despite the tired lines etching his handsome face, he lit up when he saw her.

"Hi, how's Sal doing?" he asked, like it was perfectly normal for him to be doing housework at Bernardino's.

Sofía frowned, dismayed to find him here. "What are you—"

"She was just about to fill me in," Paul interrupted. "Why don't you leave that basket on top of the dryer and come join us? I'll put those towels away later. You've done enough work already."

"Sure. Give me a sec." Nate swiveled to head back down the hall.

As soon as Sofía caught herself admiring his view from behind she turned her head away, only to find Paul taking advantage of the chance to admire the sight Nate treated them both to.

Paul shot her a knowing look, his perfectly filled in reddish-blond brows waggling playfully. Subtext—*see what I mean!* He nudged her shoulder, pushing her toward the living room with its red cushioned sofa and matching ottoman.

Sofía narrowed her eyes at him, but followed. She dropped her shoulder bag on the tile floor next to the sofa and plopped down, exhaustion catching up with her.

Nate being here threw another log into the flash fire that had become her life in the past two weeks since Lily's death. He'd broken a sort of unspoken rule between them.

In the past when he'd visited her in Key West, they'd kept to themselves. Usually he booked a room at a hotel with a sunset view, allowing them to have more privacy away from her work place. Even the one time Nate had stayed overnight with her, they'd avoided interacting with guests and the staff. Sal and Vivi had met him only because they'd run into each other at a local restaurant.

But Nate had never set foot inside the main house. She'd worked hard to keep a clear separation between her real life and the semi-fantasy world created by their occasional hook ups. Now that they didn't even have those, she didn't want to see him naturally fitting in at Bernardino's. He didn't need to be joking with her staff and winning them over. Nate wasn't around for long. Soon, he'd be off doing his father's bidding. That's how it always was with him.

Frustration welled within her, and she grabbed Paul's wrist to pull him down beside her.

"When you texted to say you had it under control after Frankie and Joy went home sick, I didn't know you meant you had recruited Nate," Sofía whispered harshly. "What were you thinking?"

"Oh, I didn't ask him to do any housework, girl." Paul slapped a silver-ringed hand to his chest. "That was all his idea. Though, I did hint at recruiting him for a little something else, but he wasn't buying what I was selling."

Paul chuckled, pleased by his own joke. Sofía slapped a hand to her forehead in dismay.

"Oh, don't fret. You know I'm fully committed to Ralphie. Your Nate and I were only having a little laugh together. Like I said, he's a good man, that one. I can see why you've been keeping him a secret."

"He's not *my* Nate," Sofía clarified. "We're...we were...well, it's complicated. But we're not together."

"Whatever you say, sweetie." Paul patted her knee with a sly grin, then leaned back on the sofa cushion and crossed his pale legs.

Before she could warn him to behave, Nate rounded the corner into the living room.

"So Sal's out of surgery, right?" he asked, settling on the ottoman angled off her end of the sofa. His knee brushed hers. Even through her black leggings, the light contact sent little sparks of awareness darting up her leg.

Sofía edged away in a bid to create more space between them.

"Yes," she answered. "Sal was in recovery when we left. The doctors recommended we give him some time to rest, so I convinced Vivi to come home, shower, and lay down for a bit before we go back."

"Poor Vivi's probably a wreck after everything she went through last night." Paul wrung his hands, frown lines marring his brow.

"She was pretty freaked out when Nate dropped me off at the hospital, but she's staying strong," Sofía said. "The doctors said we're lucky Vivi reacted so quickly by calling 911. That was crucial."

She went on to explain about Sal's two blocked arteries, which had led to his early morning angioplasty surgery and the stints that would hopefully help alleviate his chest pain and pressure. So far, he was holding his own. To be safe, they planned to keep him for the next two days and ensure there weren't any complications. Following his release from the hospital, there were some major lifestyle and eating habit changes in store for Sal. Vivi had promised to keep an eye on it.

Sofía punctuated the retelling of the events and the doctor's orders with a large yawn. Which, apparently, was contagious because Nate followed suit, covering his mouth with a fist.

"Have you gotten any sleep yet today?" she asked him.

Nate rolled his shoulders as if trying to relieve their tension. "Not yet. Paul's had his hands full."

"Less so with your large, highly capable ones around," her outspoken assistant manager threw back.

The two men grinned at the brash joke.

Dios sálvame, Sofía prayed, rolling her eyes to the heavens. But she'd been asking God to save Sal since last night, so she figured asking Him to save her from Paul's cheeky sense of humor might be too much.

"Look, you two need a break. I've got things covered. Besides, only one room is turning over here so it's all good. Go get some rest." Paul gave her thigh a quick double pat, then he pushed off the couch. "I've got some towels to put away, then I'll stroll around the corner to the other properties."

Nate covered another yawn with his fist, sending Paul a half-hearted wave with the other hand. Poor guy, he'd driven through the night, then been put straight to work.

"Paul's right," Sofía told him. "You've definitely earned a break. And if I don't get some decent sleep soon, I'll wind up passing out right where I am."

"Maybe the guests would see it as an interesting piece of live art," Nate teased, his tired eyes crinkling with his smile. "You can title it 'Chica on a Couch.'"

Sofía huffed a short laugh, waffling between happy to have him here during this scary time with Sal and worried about how seamlessly he fit into her world. Especially when she knew his father's pull would easily rip Nate out of her life again.

"I'd probably go with a title like 'Sleep Deprived,'" she suggested on a worn-out sigh.

Nate nodded, only to have it interrupted by another yawn.

"Come on," she told him. "The clock is ticking closer to four, when the doctors said Vivi and I could visit Sal again."

He reached for her hand as they rose from their seats. Instinctively, she threaded her fingers with his. Warmth from his palm seeped into hers, traveling straight to her heart. Afraid she felt too much where he was concerned, Sofía forced herself to let go, using the guise of bending down to straighten a few Florida Keys travel magazines left out for guests.

Cuidado.

The warning was a faint caution whispering in her ear. Two years ago, she'd played it off like Nate's decision to commit to another woman rather than her didn't matter. The girls had known differently. In their own ways, they'd rallied around her.

Evie, who typically texted because her work schedule kept her running most of the time, had actually called to check on her as soon as Nate and Melanie's engagement had been announced. Jenna and Lily had tried cajoling her into heading up to Paradise Key for a girls' weekend. Lauren had sent a bottle of bubbly and a box of gourmet chocolates, with a note about how getting rid of an unworthy man was a cause for celebration.

It was easier to think of Nate in Lauren's jaded divorcée terms—unworthy. But when she looked at herself in the mirror, if she was honest with herself, part of Sofía understood the reasoning behind his decision. After all, she'd turned down scholarships to out-of-state colleges and job offers on the West Coast, so she could stay close to her *familia*—especially her younger brothers who looked up to her—because she knew the importance and strength of family ties. While she believed the ones Nate's father held were the kind that choked, she would never ask Nate to risk severing them, even if it seemed like the better option. That was for him to decide.

He had. He simply hadn't chosen her.

As she led Nate down the red clay-tiled hall to the back door, Sofía assured herself that she was fine. Tía Mili had loved and lost Tío David, her soulmate, and she'd survived. Even better, she ran her own company and lived a full life with friends and *familia*.

What Sofía and Nate had shared couldn't compare to that. With her and Nate, it'd been strictly fun and games. Brief escapes from the stress of their separate lives.

While he was here or, if she made it back to Paradise Key for the Land Planning Agency meeting on Monday where interested parties were scheduled to give a brief presentation on their bid, she could do friends. At arm's length.

It was a solid plan. One she felt comfortable with. Right up until they entered her bungalow…and it hit her that the two of them would have to share her queen-sized bed.

"MAKE YOURSELF AT home," Sofía said as she ushered Nate inside.

After a quick glance around her modest bungalow, she realized he had already done so.

His duffle sat on the tile floor at the foot of her bed. His sunglasses rested on the breakfast bar next to her key bowl. His laptop and a leather folio notebook lay on the coffee table in front of the loveseat, waiting for him to get to work. Which he'd apparently neglected while helping Paul.

"Feel free to grab a snack from the fridge or pantry if you're hungry. I mean, hopefully Paul showed you around the kitchen at the main house and fed you lunch before he practically added you to the payroll. Can't believe that happened. Anyway, I'm going to wash up and then maybe—"

"Sof."

Nate said her name softly, the husky sound stopping the deluge of words tumbling uncontrollably out of her mouth.

Closing her eyes, she took a deep breath, willing herself to find the sense of calm determination that made her great at her job. As a manager, she handled the daily idiosyncrasies at three B&Bs teeming with guests and a full staff. Ask anyone and they'd confirm she was seldom ruffled, rarely uncertain, and never prone to babbling.

All three of which she currently battled.

"It's going to be okay." The confidence in his voice washed over her like a warm ocean wave, soothing her frazzled nerves. "I know you're dealing with stressful situations right now. Trying to pull your resort bid together, Sal's health scare, running the three properties on your own while he and Vivi focus on his recovery. But you've proven there's nothing you can't do. Ever. Especially with your knack for inspiring those around you. Including me."

Her next breath picked up a hint of his woodsy cologne, the musky undertone teasing her senses. Her skin prickled, alerting her to his nearness. Sofía opened her eyes to find Nate barely a step away.

Afraid she might close the distance between them and sink into the comfort he offered, despite knowing how fleeting it might be, Sofía backed up. Her shoulders bumped against the front door.

Nate stopped, his expression calm, his voice conciliatory as he put his hands palms up, facing her. "Look, no strings here. That's what you've always wanted. I get it."

Dios, could he really be that dense? After all these years, had he really not picked up on how much she cared for him?

Then again, that should be good news. Her secret was safe. Her pride intact.

"We both have full plates right now," Nate continued.

"Which is why you have no business folding towels or giving directions to the nearest bike rental shop."

"But I'm good at both of those things. Wait until your guests ask me about dinner reservation suggestions."

"No." Sofía shook her head. Sidestepping him, she strode toward the bath across from her small kitchen, on the back side of the square bungalow. "You don't need to be working behind the front desk again."

"Relegating me to dish duty already?"

"Not even that."

"Bed changing or vacuuming?"

"Stoooop!" She drew out the word as she swung around, unable to quell the smile his playfulness brought to her lips.

Nate stood by the door, hands deep in the side pockets of his khaki shorts, grinning at her.

Ay, if that look didn't weaken a girl's resolve, nothing would. She knew better, though, and wouldn't go down without a fight.

"Let's be clear with each other, all of this that's going on here is…" She moved her hands in circular motions in front of her as if she were mixing dominoes on a table top. "It's…well, I'm not sure what it is." She dropped her arms at her side, frustrated with her inability to put a label on what they were doing. "Look, I appreciate all you've done last night and today. I do. But you have your own work and responsibilities to deal with. Sal and Vivi have some big decisions to make in the wake of his heart attack. Those decisions affect me and my future. They affect Paul. They affect everyone on my staff, and I can't afford to be distracted right now."

"So I'm a distraction, huh?" His wink told her he knew he was provoking her ire. His move to pick up his laptop and settle on the loveseat also let her know he wouldn't push. "Sof, I don't have to be anywhere until Friday afternoon. If you can use some untethered help, I'm all yours."

He opened his laptop, then tapped the keyboard to illuminate his screen.

"Aren't you going to get some rest?" she asked. He had to be running on empty. She was, and she'd napped during their drive down.

"In a minute. There are a few emails I want to respond to, hit the ball back in their court." He glanced up at her for a hot second, then dropped his gaze to his laptop again. "Grab a shower. Unless things have changed, you always sleep better after a warm bath."

¡Increíble! Sofía barely kept her irritated growl from escaping.

Incredible, indeed! How was it possible for him to know what helped her relax in the evenings, yet have no clue about how much she had loved him? *Had,* because no way could she allow herself to feel that deeply or be hurt to that degree again.

Nate's absolute thick-headedness reminded her of Mami's complaint one year when Papi forgot their anniversary. "*¡Ese hombre tiene una inteligencia inmensa construyendo cosas, pero para cosas del amor, Dios me ayude!*"

Yes, Papi was incredibly intelligent when it came to building things, like Nate was with buying actual buildings. Unfortunately, both men were occasionally challenged with matters involving love. Mami's pleas for God to help her deal had been made in jest, but they'd been answered when Papi surprised her with a romantic dinner at her favorite restaurant.

At this point in her life, Sofía would choose Nate folding towels for her guests over a romantic night out. But even that made her leery.

"What?" Nate's brows met in a perplexed frown as he shot her a confused look, and she realized she'd wasted several minutes blankly staring at him typing away on his keyboard.

"Um, nothing." She shook her head, trying to wake her brain from its stupor. "Just thinking about a few things I need to check before we head back to the hospital."

"Okay," he mumbled, already lost again in whatever he'd started reading.

Without another word, Sofía grabbed a change of clothes from her dresser along the left front wall, dropped her tote bag on the breakfast bar, then hit the bath.

Minutes later, after not nearly long enough under the warm shower spray, she threw on a comfortable tee and black leggings. Removing the claw clip from her hair so it wouldn't bug her when she napped, she left the bathroom.

"Are you sure you're not hungry—" Sofía broke off as soon as she saw Nate, chin dropped to his chest, fast asleep still sitting upright on the couch, his laptop propped in front of him.

Relaxed, the tired lines smoothed from his handsome face, making him appear younger. Almost vulnerable—a word he probably wouldn't choose to define himself.

As much as he talked about all that she juggled, she knew he was in the same position. Expectations, responsibilities, personal goals, and a slew of people depending on them.

Only, she didn't have a hard-ass father poking and prodding and picking at her every move.

No, she had Papi, always supportive and quick to tell her how proud he was of her. And Sal, a father-figure in his own way. Both were men who'd give anybody the shirt off their backs. Unlike Nathan's dad, who found fault with nearly everything his son did and was more prone to write someone a check to go buy their own shirt, as if his money was the solution to everything.

Nathan Hamilton, II, rarely acknowledged his son's brilliance. Oftentimes, Sofía felt his father's shadow loomed too large over Nate, making it difficult for him to forge his own way. He deserved better.

As if sensing the agitation churning within her, Nate stirred. His computer shifted, in danger of sliding off his lap.

Basta, she chided herself, enough fretting over a situation she couldn't change. If she didn't get Nate to lie down, he'd wind up with a crick in his neck and his back out of sorts. That was no way to thank him for all his help.

"Nate, come on," she whispered, moving his laptop and setting it next to the tropical-scented candle on her coffee table. She put a hand on his shoulder to give him a gentle shake. "Let's move you to the bed."

"Um-hmm, join me." His drowsy attempt at a sexy grin wound up making him look more like a mischievous little boy.

Sofía chuckled—always working an angle, this one.

"Easy," she murmured when he stumbled into her trying to rise from the loveseat.

One hand on his forearm, the other wrapped around his waist, she guided him to the bed. Her pulse picked up its pace, her body tingling in places it shouldn't at the idea of sleeping next to him again.

"Here you go." She eased him down on the mattress edge, and he collapsed onto her duvet.

Rolling on his side, he burrowed his head and shoulder into the pillow. Within seconds, he was asleep, his lips curving at whatever pleasure danced in his dreams.

Sofía slipped off his Sperrys, then rounded the bed to gingerly lie down beside him. Mimicking Nate's position, she rolled onto her left shoulder to face him. She reached out, leaving her hand hovering in the air between them.

Longing pierced her chest, a cascade of pleasure-pain rippling through her.

Ay, she imagined her fingertips brushing across his forehead, down his chiseled cheekbones, along his square jaw, and around the outline of his full lips. Feeling what she'd only imagined in her mind in the long months since they'd last seen each other. Tasting what she'd robbed herself of by holding to her principles.

But she didn't trust herself to stop with a simple touch. Not when her body remembered the flare of passion and how amazing it had always been between them. Nate took her to heights she'd never reached with another man. Part of her feared it would always be that way for her.

And yet, she missed more than just the sex. It was like he reached her on a different level. Nate had almost always been there for her during her darkest times—when she'd called bullshit on the owners of the South Beach resort after they'd promoted their idiot nephew instead of her and she'd threatened to quit, when Abuela suffered her stroke and passed away before Sofía could get to Puerto Rico to say good-bye, and now all of this.

Unfortunately, "all of this" was worse than Nate even knew.

Her bid for the resort was in real jeopardy. No way could she expect Sal to jump into another business proposition considering the stress involved. Vivi had mentioned wanting them to get out of the B&B business, fully retire.

Sofía was scared. Not only was she facing the loss of her dream to own the resort, but also potentially the loss of her current job. Her throat tightened with unshed tears—of frustration and disappointment. But she refused to let them fall. They wouldn't do any good.

She needed to talk options out with someone. In the past, that would have been Sal or Nate. Her mentor wasn't an option this time. Maybe…

Maybe she needed to stop fighting Nate, and herself. Stop pushing away the help he offered. If they couldn't be what she had once hoped, maybe friendship and mutual support could be enough. Certainly better than the nothing she'd had over the past two years.

Satisfied with her logic, or at least trying to convince herself she was, Sofía placed her hand over Nate's on the duvet between them. A sense of calm seeped over her as her eyes closed.

She drifted to sleep, strengthened by their connection. Relieved to have him beside her. At least for now.

Chapter Nine

NATE WOKE TO the incredible sensation of Sofía's warm body pressed against his side, her head resting on his chest. Her spicy floral scent teased and excited him, the same way Sofía did whenever he was around her. Or thought of her.

His cell buzzed in his shorts pocket. Thankfully it stopped almost as soon as it started indicating he'd received a text message. Moving as little as possible to avoid rousing Sofía, since she needed her sleep and he needed to keep her at his side as long as possible, he dug out his phone.

One-handed, he pecked out his security code with his left thumb, then tapped the message icon to see his father's name at the top of the list, followed by two other key players involved with the Sarasota property. Those should take priority, but his father would continue hammering away like an annoying woodpecker if Nate didn't respond.

Where the hell are you?

Kind of close to *how the hell are you.* A guy could almost say his dad was showing how much he cared. Yeah, right.

Nate smirked, his thumb doing gymnastics across the

small screen as he typed.

Off the grid. Working deals. It's all good.

His father hated it when Nate tossed out that phra—

Cut the crap and foolishness. Don't make me send someone else to do your job.

Damn, the man had a knack for interrupting him even when they weren't face to face. It took talent. Or ego.

Nate sighed. The rise and fall of his chest on the disgruntled breath had Sofía snuggling closer. Her dark hair tickled his chin, and he moved his right hand to stroke the silky tresses.

As much as he wanted to stay here being a pillow for her, duty called. He needed to follow up with his Sarasota contacts. Fingers crossed his gamble would pay off.

Supporting Sofía's head with one hand, Nate slid out from under her, deftly replacing his body with the king-sized pillow he'd been laying on.

Sofía mumbled a complaint. She stretched in her sleep, the motion pulling her peach T-shirt taut over her full breasts. Settling back to sleep, she crooked a knee, giving him an enticing view of her shapely butt and thighs in her sexy black leggings. Her fuchsia-painted toes were a splash of color against the cream-colored duvet. The same way she and her personality added a splash of color in what had been a dull life without her the past two years.

Blood coursed low in Nate's body, his response instinctive and swift, as it always was when it came to her. And only her. When he'd been a randy teen, he had struggled with how to control his physical reaction to her. Not wanting to risk moving too fast.

Back then, he'd chalked it up to youthful hormones. Though as time went by and his attraction only intensified, he'd come to realize it was much more than that. Everything about Sofía drew him. Excited him. Comforted him. Made him want to be better.

His phone vibrated again, reminding Nate he hadn't responded to his father's latest not-so-veiled threat.

Padding over to the fridge to grab a bottle of water, he paused to type.

Nice try. No one else can handle what I'm putting together for our company. Working on final details & will send when I'm ready. I'll be in touch.

Subtext—*stop henpecking.* Not that his father had ever been any good at subtext. Or caring about it, anyway.

Then, because he hadn't called his mom in a few days, Nate fired off a message to her.

I'm helping a friend & working a few business angles. Tell him to back off. Will call you soon. Love.

Pressing the side button to lock his screen, Nate slid his phone back into his pocket. He reached for the black plastic handle on the side-by-side fridge door, but paused when his gaze caught on a red magnetic photo frame with five cutouts for pictures. He slid his gaze from one photo to the other, each depicting a facet of the *familia* Sofía held dear.

The first captured her with the four other girls when they were in their late teens, hanging out by the pool at Paradise Key Resort. The Fabulous Five-some. So different from each other in looks and personality, yet closer than many sisters.

There was a recent pic of Sofía, her parents, and two younger brothers. The Spanish fort *El Morro* in Old San Juan and the expansive grassy area surrounding it behind them. Arms around each other, huge grins splitting their tanned faces.

Another showed Sofía, Sal, and Vivi at a local Cuban restaurant on Mallory Square where tourists flocked to admire the famous Key West sunset.

A fourth, older picture, had a young Sofía, arms around Tía Mili and a man Nate recognized was her late husband Tío David enjoying a family picnic at some park. Probably in Miami where Mili and David had lived before moving to Paradise Key.

The final space was empty. Either a photo recently removed or the spot yet to be filled.

Nate knew whose picture he wanted to slide between the magnetic frame and the fridge. One of him and Sofía. Another facet of her *familia* tableau. But that wasn't his decision to make.

Of course, that didn't mean he couldn't do everything in

his power to convince her he was worth taking a chance on again.

For that to happen, he had to get to work.

After snagging a water bottle from the fridge, he picked up his laptop and leather notebook, then headed outside to make some calls.

Nate opened the door, nearly running into the raised fist of a slim guy with curly black hair and darkly tanned skin. The man, who looked about Nate's age, sported a short-sleeved white linen shirt over baggy olive pants. Either he'd gotten dressed in a hurry and missed the top three buttons or he wanted to make sure onlookers noticed the metal crucifix dangling from a thin leather strap that hit him square in the center of his chest. Based on the scowl pulling the guy's dark brows in an angry slant, he was as surprised to find Nate exiting Sofía's house as Nate was to see this Lothario looka-like about to knock.

"You overshot your destination, buddy. The main guest-house is over there." Nate gestured to the three-story Victorian.

"I am aware of that." The man's thick Spanish accent highlighted the sneer in his voice. "I am here to see Sofía. Who are you?"

"I'm her—"

"Nate, who's there?" Sofía's groggy call had Nate glancing back over his shoulder at her. Unfortunately, the move gave the guy a chance to push his way into the bungalow.

"¿Sofía, porque no haz contestado mis llamadas?"

At least that was good news. Apparently, whoever this guy was, Sofía hadn't bothered returning his calls. Nate liked the sound of that.

"Franco, what are you doing here?" Sitting up on the edge of her bed, Sofía brushed her hair out of her face, a perplexed frown creasing her forehead.

The guy's suspicious gaze flicked over Nate, who stepped back inside and closed the door behind him. He wasn't the interloper here, so he wasn't going anywhere.

Continuing in Spanish, Franco claimed to have heard about Sal and assumed Sofía would want his comfort. The guy probably thought speaking in her native tongue would shut Nate out. His thought would be wrong.

Nate had enrolled in Spanish his junior year after meeting Sofía that first summer, then continued classes all four years in college. After graduation, he'd whisked Sofía off to Barcelona where they'd spent two glorious weeks eating, drinking, sightseeing, and practicing his Spanish. Among other activities.

He was the Hamilton their business partners in the Caribbean spoke with regularly, not his father.

"I'm fine. Sal's the one to worry about." Sofía pushed herself to a stand. Hands on her curvy hips, she quirked one side of her mouth with resignation. The move drew attention to her sexy beauty mark.

As much as Nate relished dreaming about kissing that

mole again, the last thing Sofía needed was a second idiot thinking more about what he wanted than what was best for her.

"*Mi amor*—"

"Franco, I told you that this wasn't going to work out." Sofía crossed to the breakfast bar that separated the tiny kitchen area from the living space. "Right after you complained because I wasn't going to be in town to watch you compete in the Battle of the Chefs due to one of my best friend's funeral."

"That was shock and grief talking, *no?*"

Nate scoffed, quickly turning it into a cough at Franco's glare.

"You would give us the privacy, *okay?*"

Franco switched to English, directing his question at Nate, who couldn't care less what the chef or cook or whatever this guy was wanted. He'd take his cues from Sofía; she was the one who mattered here.

When Nate looked to her for direction, she had already grabbed her tote bag and slung its strap over her shoulder. The keys dangling from one of her fingers made it clear to him that Sofía wasn't interested in continuing the conversation. Privately or not.

"I'm sorry, but I don't have time for this right now, Franco." She shook her head, her expression more resigned than angry. Which, Nate knew, was worse. Angry might blow over after she vented, usually in a mix of Spanish and

English fondly called Spanglish. Resigned meant the cold shoulder or, if it was really bad, the wall of silence.

Sofía strode toward the door, not waiting for her friend—a description Nate used because he refused to think about her actually dating this yahoo—to respond. "Vivi's already texted to see if I'm on my way to pick her up so we can keep Sal company this evening. I have to go."

"And this one, he will stay here?" Franco waved a dismissive hand in Nate's direction.

Okay, "this one" was starting to get a little pissed.

"Yes, he's here until Friday," Sofía answered. "Helping me and the staff."

Nate tried...granted, not very hard, the guy was a chump...but he couldn't quite squelch his smug grin at her words. He'd fallen asleep earlier with her not even wanting him to pull kitchen duty. Whatever had changed her mind, he was grateful.

"You do not want to make this mistake, *querida*." Adding the *beloved* endearment did nothing to soften Franco's egotistical warning. If anything, it made things worse.

Jerking her wrist to swing her keys around her finger, Sofía caught them in her fist. Her hazel eyes flashed with annoyance. "We were professional acquaintances before we started seeing each other, Franco. And a few dates isn't really... Look, let's not say anything to damage that professional relationship. I respect you, and I admire your talent. It's why Bernardino's recommends your restaurant to our guests. But do not disrespect me by thinking you can tell me what to do in my own home. Or in my place of business."

Her clipped words and the steel undercurrent left no doubt about her displeasure.

Franco tilted his head in assent, his expression grim. "*Perdóname.*"

Nate might have felt bad for the guy, if Franco's apology hadn't come after he'd acted like a complete ass while making a move on Sofía right in front of him. And if waking up from his nap with her in his arms hadn't given Nate a sliver of hope.

"If you'd like to walk me to my car, Franco, I'll fill you in on Sal's prognosis." Sofía opened the front door, moving aside for the chef to precede her out.

Nate listened to the other man clomp down the wooden steps without even a good-bye.

"Thank you," Sofía called from the open doorway. The afternoon sun streamed in behind her, casting a long shadow across the bungalow's mottled cream tile floor.

"For what?" Nate asked.

"Not rising to his bait."

Nate lifted a shoulder in a blasé shrug. "Anything for you, Sof."

And he meant it.

Head quirked to the side, as if considering him or his words, maybe both, she eyed him for a few quiet beats. Nate sat on the loveseat and opened his laptop, like it was no big deal for him to be here, in her home, working on a deal that could change her life, and potentially his, too.

"I should be back in a few hours. If you haven't eaten, maybe we can grab a late dinner?" she asked.

"Sounds like a plan."

Her lips curved at his response. She wiggled her fingers in farewell, then closed the door behind her.

In the silence that followed her departure, Nate's gaze traveled around her bungalow, taking in the personal touches that made this tiny space a home. The photographs peppering surfaces, from her dresser to the end table, from the wall above the loveseat to the fridge, they all captured favorite memories with her beloved *familia*. The white-framed print over her bed depicted a rushing waterfall and lush vegetation in *El Yunque*, the Puerto Rican rain forest she'd hiked and swam in as a kid. On the counter to the left of the gas stove sat two cookbooks. One was filled with her Abuela's handwritten recipes; the other was purchased during their Barcelona trip. It was the only tie to him that he could see. He wanted to change that.

His place in New York was three or four times bigger than the bungalow. It had city views and professional interior design style. It was in a fantastic location with amazing food and drink options within walking distance. But it lacked one important aspect, one important person. Sofía.

For him, this place felt more like home because she was here. There wasn't anywhere else he wanted to be.

For any chance at making this permanent, he had to put everything into his effort.

Pulling his phone from his shorts pocket, Nate hit the "call back" button for one of his Sarasota contacts.

"Hi Saul, it's Nate Hamilton. I'm hoping you've got some good news for me regarding the geotechnical and hydrology studies. I'm ready to make someone's dream come true."

"YES, NATE'S STILL here," Sofía said into her phone as she walked along Front Street toward the heart of downtown Key West. "He's staying with me until Friday morning."

"Damn." Evie's muttered curse on the other end of the line was pretty much the reaction Sofía had expected when she had informed the girls via text that Nate was in Key West with her.

Of course, Sofía had thought she'd see the word from Evie in their group message thread, not hear it live.

Jenna had responded with all shouty caps.

WHAT?!?!

Ever the cynical one when it came to men, Lauren had chimed in.

Be careful. Don't let him fool you.

Not surprising since Lauren had rightfully earned that suspicious streak thanks to her recent divorce, but Jenna's answer to the warning had taken Sofía by surprise.

Yeah, men aren't all they're cracked up to be.

Worried by the jaded comment from the most nonconfrontational of the bunch, Sofía fired off a return text.

Are you okay, Jen?

All she'd gotten back was a thumbs-up icon. No explanation. *Dios*, with everything else so freaking topsy-turvy in their lives, Sofía hoped there wasn't some kind of trouble between sweet Jenna and her easygoing boyfriend.

Evie, on the other hand, had remained suspiciously silent in the thread. Then, moments after the chatter quieted, her name had flashed across Sofía's cell screen, indicating a call.

"You sure about this?" Evie asked now.

Hearing the concern in her friend's voice, Sofía pressed the phone to her ear, as if it would bring them closer. She glanced to her right and left, checking for oncoming traffic before crossing at the corner of Duval and Front Street. The downtown area swarmed with tourists, most heading in the same direction, Sunset Pier.

She had arrived home from the hospital about fifteen minutes ago to find a note from Nate on the breakfast bar in her bungalow.

Headed to Mallory Square to catch sunset with a few

129

guests.

Let me know if you're still up for dinner.

—Nate

"I tell you, girl, the man's a keeper," Paul had teased when she'd gone back to the main house to ask how long ago Nate and the group had left.

"Did you hear me?" Evie asked, when Sofía hadn't answered.

Sidestepping a young couple exiting the Starbucks on the corner, Sofía quickened her pace.

"Yes. I'm thinking," she said. "I'm…I'm as sure as I can be with so much of my life up in the air right now."

"That's what I'm worried about. I know your pride won't admit this, but make sure you're not trying to hold onto the past. What you and Nate had back when it was the five of us ready to take on the world. I don't want you to get hurt again, Sof."

"Me either."

She took a right onto narrow Exchange Street. A short block ahead sat the parking lot at Mallory Square, next to the large building that housed El Mesón de Pepe. The Cuban restaurant was always a good choice for dinner. The outdoor seating area allowed patrons to enjoy the live Latin music and dancing on the wide brick-lined sidewalk, with views of the ocean and Sunset Key behind them. Inside seating offered more privacy along with a brightly painted walk-through museum depicting the history of Cuba and Key

West.

"I'm going into this wide-eyed, without blinders. Promise."

"Good," Evie said. "Nate's a good guy, Sof. But his family isn't like yours. *Familia*, like you talk about, dads like your papi, aren't the norm for people like Nate and me. We don't have that. And it really messes with you."

"I know," Sofía murmured. Something in Evie's voice touched a warning signal in the back of Sofía's mind.

Reaching the parking lot next to El Mesón de Pepe's building, she slowed her steps. If she went much farther, it'd be difficult to hear her phone conversation.

Ahead of her, a crowd of tourists and locals packed Mallory Square. Jugglers, a bagpipe player in a Scottish kilt, acrobats, live statues with silver painted bodies, and other street performers wowed onlookers. Vendors set up with easy tear-down booths worked at selling their island-themed wares. Behind them all, like a cinematic backdrop, the bright sun blazed in a ball of fire, shooting blood-orange flames that bled across the horizon as it raced to disappear in the ocean.

"Is there something going on with you, Evie?" *Dios mío*, were any of them in a peaceful place right now? Jenna might or might not be having man trouble. Lauren had confessed to issues at work. Sofía's resort bid and maybe even her job at Bernardino's, if Sal and Vivi decided to sell and head back north, were at risk.

"You have your own issues to stress over. I'll be fine."

Evie's brush-off didn't convince Sofía. If anything, it cranked her concerns up a notch. But she wasn't the only one in their group with a streak of pride as wide as the Gulf of Mexico. Evie would share when she was ready.

"*Bueno*, you know I'm here," Sofía said.

"Always."

They hung up, each promising to stay in touch. Then, with the sun steadfastly sinking in the sky, Sofía tapped out a text asking Nate where he and the guests were located on the Square.

A few minutes later, she wove her way through a group gathered around a pair of acrobats, one balancing on the shoulders of another who straddled a unicycle. Off to the right, she spotted Nate hanging on the outskirts of the oohing and aahing audience, watching a juggler's talent with black and red bowling pins.

Casually dressed in loose-fitting, pale blue cotton shorts, a grey fitted tee, and his tan Sperrys, his face beaming with laughter at whatever the juggler joked about, Nate looked relaxed, happy. He turned, as if he sensed her watching him, and his green eyes brightened even more when he saw her.

His reaction to her arrival made her heart actually flutter in her chest. The love for him she had desperately tried to bury over the last two years swelled, consuming her like a flood of molten lava.

Nate reached out to her. Because she couldn't not take what he offered, Sofía hurried forward to clasp his hand with hers.

He linked their fingers, tugging her closer and bending down to brush a kiss on her cheek. She closed her eyes briefly, savoring the warmth of his lips on her skin.

"It's good to see you," he said, the quick squeeze of his hand punctuating his words.

"I'm glad I made it before sunset."

"Sal still improving?"

She nodded. "They're talking about releasing him tomorrow."

The crowd's cheers over the juggler's last trick interrupted their conversation. They joined the applause, then moved with the family from the guesthouse to sit on the pier's cement wall and marvel at nature's watercolor sky.

Sofía and Nate had watched Key West sunsets in the past—here on Mallory Square, from the balcony of his hotel suite, once from the deck of a private sailboat. But tonight felt different. She felt different.

Almost like...like they were on borrowed time.

For these next few days could she pretend that things between them were good again? She was already allowing herself to rely on him for help with Bernardino's. She might even risk talking to him about her bid and her options, few though they were.

Maybe she'd even completely let down her guard, be with him in the way she craved.

All while knowing that when he left for his meeting on

Friday, they'd return to opposite sides, vying for Paradise Key Resort. He'd be firmly back in the Hamilton camp, with his father as ring leader.

If she did like she'd promised Evie, go in without blinders knowing the outcome, she'd be okay.

The sun disappeared while she wrestled with the swirl of her what-if thoughts. With night falling, the crowd started dispersing. Some wandered back to hotel rooms after a day in the sun. Others walked to local restaurants for dinner. Many were off to hit the bars lining Duval Street.

The B&B guests, a husband and wife with their teen daughter who were visiting from upstate New York, asked where they could find some good Cuban food. Together, they all headed back toward El Mesón de Pepe. Outside, on a two-foot high stage that was enclosed on three sides, the restaurant's regular three-man salsa band had already started a set. An older couple well into their sixties showed off their dance moves on the brick-lined dance area, much to the diners' pleasure.

Sofía and Nate made sure the family knew how to get back to the guesthouse, then parted ways with them, opting to sit at El Mesón de Pepe's patio bar rather than wait for a table. They ordered the restaurant's signature Cuban nachos, made with plantain chips and a mix of *ropa vieja* and *picadillo*. Nate practically salivated in anticipation of the Cuban shredded flank steak and ground beef topped with guacamole, onions, and cheese.

While they waited for their food to arrive, he sipped on a whiskey straight and Sofía stirred the mini straw in her rum and Diet Coke. The band finished a fast-paced merengue, then transitioned into a sexy Prince Royce bachata. The young singer with Dominican roots was a regular on Sofía's playlist, never failing to make her shoulders and hips sway to his sultry beats. Eyes closed, she reveled in the sensory nirvana created by the seductive music, warm ocean breeze, and tasty cuisine fresh from the kitchen. For the first time since the call about Lily, a sense of peace warmed her soul. Thanks in large part to the man beside her.

Nate set his glass on the wood bar, then rose and held his arm out to her, palm up. "Dance with me?"

The sexy arch of his brow, the hopeful glint in his eyes, and the playful quirk of his lips made a devastating combination. No way could she turn him down.

"Think you can keep up with me?" Sofía teased.

"You'd be surprised. I had a pretty decent instructor. Two actually."

She chuckled, but it quickly turned into a bark of laughter at his wink.

"Yes, you did."

Dios, the dance lessons she and Tía Mili had given him in the condo living room over that first summer seemed like eons ago. He'd come over for dinner, and she and Tía Mili had music playing in the background as they danced around the kitchen together. Tía Mili reminisced about the parties she and Mami had attended as young girls, when they'd met Papi and Tío David.

Nate had surprised them by asking if they'd teach him how to dance. Sofía swore that was the night he won over Tía Mili. A *gringo* shimmying his hips, awkwardly at first, quick to laugh at his missteps. Eventually easing into the motions of the salsa and merengue.

The bachata, like the one playing now, had come later, when there hadn't been a chaperone. When it'd just been the two of them, bodies pressed together, learning how to move as one. A promise of what would come. When they were both ready.

Nate led her across the bricked dancing area to the edge of the light shining from the patio bar, where they could dance in the half shadows. She moved into his open arms, awareness sizzling through her when he placed his right palm between the small of her back and her left hip, guiding her closer. Sliding one hand behind his right shoulder, she laid her other in his open palm in a dancer's hold.

"You ready for this?" Nate whispered in her ear.

Her pulse sparked, excitement and desire flaring in secret parts of her body.

"Show me what you've got."

Laughter rumbled in his chest, carrying into hers.

They waited a few beats, then his gentle pressure on her hip signaled for her to start along with him. With one thigh tucked snuggly between his, their hips and upper bodies pressed together, they followed the sensuous rhythm. Swaying, undulating, moving beautifully, like always, as one.

Sofía buried her face in his neck, breathed deeply of his musky cologne. His palm slid from her hip to the center of her back, leaving a trail of heat in its wake. Her breath hitched as he bent her backward in a deep, circular dip that had her hair skimming the brick at their feet. Her hold tightened on his shoulders, at the same time the rest of her body remained fluid, allowing the gentle pressure from his hands and hips to guide her. She was putty in his arms. Willingly.

Because she trusted him.

The song ended, but neither of them released their close hold on the other. Somehow, they had drifted further into the shadows and now stood sandwiched between the broad palm trees lining the walkway and the right side of the enclosed stage.

"God, I've missed this," Nate said, his husky voice tickling her ear.

"Nate, I'm—"

"I know. I don't have any right to say that," he interrupted, mistaking her words as a cry for him to back off.

He stared down at her, the play of shadow and light accentuating his angular features. The pain clouding his eyes pierced her heart.

"I'm sorry, Sof. I messed up before; I know that now. I'm only hoping you can forgive me for—"

"Shhh," she murmured, placing her fingertips over his lips.

Tucking his chin, Nate pressed his forehead to hers. Their warm breath mingled in the tiny space between them.

"I'm going to make things right for you," he promised.

But she knew that wasn't something he could guarantee. They did, however, have the next few days together. "How about if we only think about right now? Forget about everything else and give ourselves the rest of the week."

Nate drew back, his hands falling to rest on her hips. A tiny V of confusion creased between his brows. "What do you mean?"

"Once you leave, who knows how everything is going to play out. But between now and Friday, maybe…"

Dios mío, could she do this and not get hurt again?

But she was already hurting. Why cheat herself out of something great when it was right in front of her? All she had to do was grab onto it.

"Maybe, we enjoy being with each other here. Knowing that come Monday, we can't…it'll be too…" She trailed off, overcome by the very real idea that they would be on opposite sides. Any chance of a relationship gone. For good this time.

"Don't give up on us," he demanded, his voice a desperate plea.

"It's not that simple. If I lose, I'll be devastated," Sofía admitted.

She cupped his cheek, lovingly stroked his strong jaw. Nate leaned into her touch, turning his head to kiss her palm. Longing and regret clogged her throat and she swallowed hard, struggling to push it down, back into a dark corner of her soul.

"If you lose, who knows how your father will react. I don't want to be a part of that negativity. Not aga—" She broke off, unwilling to hurt him by revealing the bribe his father had offered all those years ago. That secret would remain hers. She refused to be the one who created a wedge between him and his *familia*.

"Whatever happens with the resort shouldn't define us," he argued.

"That place. It's not just business to me. You know that." Elbows crooked, she flattened her palms on his chest and stared up at him, desperate for him to understand.

Nate's eyes drifted closed. His soft sigh released a warm puff of whiskey-tinged air that caressed her face.

Heart pounding a fast bongo beat, she whispered, "Can we forget about what might happen on Monday and just be together for the next few days?"

"And then?"

Tears stung her eyes. She lifted her shoulders in a desolate shrug, trying to smile, but failing miserably. "I don't want to think beyond right now. Can we not do that?"

Behind them, the band struck up the notes of another sexy bachata. A determined expression tightened Nate's features as he stared off into the darkened area of Mallory Square and the open ocean behind them.

"Nate?" she whispered, anxious for him to answer. Praying he'd agree to her terms.

He looked down at her, his face difficult to read in the mottled shadows. His fingers flexed on her hips and desire sparked through her, shooting straight to her core. He dipped his head toward her. Paused. Sofía's breath caught in her throat when his gaze drifted down to her mouth, then back up to meet hers again, as if waiting for her to give him some sign. Some reassurance.

She didn't need to be asked twice.

Rising onto her toes, she slid her arms around his neck, drawing his head closer. She captured his mouth with hers, his muffled groan vibrating against her lips.

His hands slid down to cradle her butt, pressing her lower body intimately against his as he deepened their kiss. The tip of his tongue flicked against her lips, and she opened for him. He tasted like fine whiskey and sin. A heady combination that had her arching her body against his, wanting, needing more.

Her fingers splayed in the short hair at his nape. Teased the shell of his ear. Everything around them faded as she reveled in the feel, the taste, the scent of this man who was everything she'd always wanted. But whom fate wouldn't allow.

A loud bark of laughter broke through Sofía's desire-fogged brain, reminding her they weren't alone. Though partially hidden by the vegetation and shadows, tourists and locals strolled nearby, with diners and waitstaff around the corner in front of the stage.

Reluctantly she broke their kiss, then leaned against Nate, pressing her face in the crook of his neck. He turned them so his back faced any onlookers, his hands tracing up her spine to cradle her shoulder blades, as if protecting her from those around them.

"You wanna get out of here?" he murmured in her ear before pressing a kiss on her temple.

She nodded. More than ready for them to have some privacy.

"Let's go home," he said, hooking an arm around her shoulders.

Sofía looped both her arms around his waist, nestling close to his side. Nate kissed the top of her head, and a warm sensation of absolute rightness rushed through her.

Home. With Nate.

Dios, she liked the sound of that.

Chapter Ten

SOFÍA TIPTOED FROM the bathroom, bending to snag one of Nate's T-shirts from the top of his duffle bag. The scent of his cologne lingered on his shirt, enveloping her as she slipped it over her head.

At the foot of her bed, she stopped, watching Nate sleep as the soft glow of moonlight filtering through the window bathed him. *Dios mío*, she didn't think she'd ever tire of this view. The measured rise and fall of his muscular chest, his handsome face relaxed, lips slightly open, their edges curved at whatever dream played in his mind.

Anxious to be near him, she crawled back in bed, tugged the covers up around them, then snuggled against his side. Nate shifted, turning to wrap an arm around her waist.

"Mm, you feel good," he murmured.

He nuzzled her neck, sending pinpricks of awareness marching down her chest.

"I'm sorry, I didn't mean to wake you," she answered.

"And miss this?" His palm skimmed her hip, down her thigh, then back again in a sensual tease.

Desire flared at his touch, and she rocked her lower body closer instinctively seeking his.

Nate gently nipped her chin with his teeth, then dropped a feather-light kiss to the same spot. Trailing kisses along her jaw, he reached her ear where he blew a warm breath that raised goose bumps on her skin. She pressed closer, seeking more of him.

"Sleep is overrated anyway," he whispered.

She chuckled. "That's good since we haven't had much the past two nights."

"I'd take this." He laved her earlobe with his warm tongue. "And this." Teased her with a kiss above her beauty mark, near the corner of her mouth. "And this."

Finally, his lips covered hers in a soul-stirring kiss. She moaned her approval, her tongue brushing against his. He caressed her hip, his hand slowly moving to cup her breast. She arched back, her nipples pebbling at his attention.

As if sensing her plea, he bent to suckle her through his shirt. A gasp escaped her throat as the heated moisture sent need arrowing down to her core.

"You're so beautiful," Nate murmured.

He pressed an open-mouthed kiss along her neck, then propped himself on his elbow to look at her.

Brushing her hair out of her face, Sofía stared up at him. Nate's sleep and desire heavy eyes locked with hers. He mimicked her move, combing his fingers through her tresses. The gentle, almost loving gesture affected her as deeply as his strokes along the more intimate places of her body.

"I've missed you," he said, his voice a gruff whisper.

"More importantly, I owe you an apology, Sof."

His words, though more than likely meant to soothe her, had Sofía drawing back to avoid them.

"We don't have to do this." Shaking her head, she pushed herself to sit up. Afraid to talk about the past. Scared to think about the future. "What's done is done."

Grabbing her pillow, she shoved it against the headboard to lean against it.

Nate sat up, too. The cream-colored sheet falling to his waist. The dips and planes of his bare torso begged her to run her hands over their expanse. Stubbornly, she fisted her hands in her lap.

"Don't shut me out, Sofía. I've been stumbling over these words, the same painful thoughts scrambling my brain, since the last time we were together. Here, in Key West."

Anger, fueled by hurt, flashed in her belly. "I don't really want to talk about another woman while we're in bed together."

"Fair enough." Tossing the sheet aside, Nate rose in all his naked glory. He stepped into a pair of boxers, but didn't bother with a shirt. Instead, he strode to the loveseat where he plopped down, arms crossed, his firm biceps flexing with the motion.

"Well, are you going to join me?" he asked when she hadn't moved.

"Nate—"

"You asked for us to give each other these days together.

Those were your terms. Mine is that we not continue with this hanging over us. This unspoken elephant in the room."

She eyed him warily, trying to decide if this was an argument she could win. Ultimately, the mix of determination and anxiety swimming in his green eyes had Sofía sliding out of bed. Rather than sit with him on the cozy loveseat, she chose a stool at the breakfast bar. Needing the distance as a buffer.

The pain she'd felt when Nate had opted to go along with his father's request was still fresh. A wound that still felt raw and unhealed. Despite the two years that had passed.

Nate started to stand. Sofía held a hand up to stop him. He tensed, but ultimately sank back onto the loveseat.

"Okay, you need some space," he acquiesced.

The fact he knew her well enough to understand that when she was upset, she either pulled back, draping a protective shield around herself so she could regroup, or she turned to loved ones for support, weakened her resolve to separate herself from him.

And yet…somehow, he hadn't known how badly his decision to propose to another woman would hurt her?

That thought kept Sofía glued to her stool, no matter how badly she wanted to go to Nate. Have him wrap his strong arms around her and promise everything would work out.

"The last time I was here, when I came to tell you about my father's ultimatum of propose to Melanie or risk being removed from the company, my head was a mess," Nate admitted.

That made two of them.

He rubbed a hand through his hair, tousling it even more. The move gave him a rumpled look that seemed to mesh with the jumble of troubled emotions swarming around and through them both.

"If you want the God's honest truth, with none of those lies of omission you've always warned me against…" he said. "I flew down here hoping you would tell me to say no."

Sofía gasped, shocked by his admission. Shocked and angered at the same time.

"Nate, you can't put that on *me*," she cried. "It's not fair."

"I know. I realize that now. Back then, though? I was scared." He shook his head. Even in the moonlit shadows, she noted his abject misery.

His easy acceptance of his failure sucked the wind out of her debate sail, deflating her ire.

"I should have stood up to my father. And Melanie's. For you and me, and for her. She was miserable. I was miserable. Hell, misery, a sense of duty, and our long-standing friendship are pretty much all Melanie and I shared. Well…" He lifted an arm, then let it fall back onto his lap. "That and the secret about her reconnecting with an old boyfriend she couldn't quite get over. Talk about two people stuck on a sinking ship. Ha!"

His bark of laughter was more disdain than mirth.

He rose to pace the short length of her living area, from the far wall near the bed's headboard, back to the love seat, then spinning on his heel to make the loop again.

The other day, he'd pointed out what he called her tells. The signs that clued him in when she was frustrated, upset, or angry. His tell was pacing while his mind worked to sort out one problem or another. Like now.

"It was unconscionable. My father issuing his ultimatum. My mom backing him up on it. Her? Of all people?" He flung his arms out as if at a loss for words.

But his pacing continued, indicating he wasn't done.

Sofía watched him battle with whatever demons ruled his thoughts right now. She wanted to go to him, stop the frantic pacing by taking him into her arms. Damn his father for causing this turmoil in the son who only wanted to make him proud.

And yet, Nate was also the man who'd broken her heart. Caused one of the biggest losses of her life. The loss of belief in herself. For a moment, until the girls had knocked some sense into her, Sofía had doubted her worth. Because she had put so much faith in Nate.

That couldn't happen again.

So she stayed on her stool. Torn between comforting the only man she had loved and protecting herself.

"How could my mom, who has lived in a loveless marriage most of her adult life, have urged me to do the same?"

Elbows bent, fists balled in front of him, Nate swung away from the far wall, striding back toward the coffee table.

Suddenly, he veered left, toward Sofía.

"But the real mistake is on me." He stopped a few feet away from her. Self-reproach stamped his features in a stark mask of pain.

Her breath trapped in her chest, Sofía felt tears prick her eyes.

"You were the best thing in my life, Sof. The one person I could always count on to be real. And I let you down."

"You hurt me."

He flinched at her quiet admission.

Inside, she did, too. Her words didn't come easily. Admitting a weakness had never been her strong suit. But he needed to know how his decision had affected her. Because he was right; if she wanted to truly get the most out of these last few days together, she had to be honest with him, too.

"Part of me understands," she continued. "I'd do anything for my *familia*. And I would never say or do anything that would pit you against yours."

Her pulse hiccupped at the thought of the hateful secret she kept. The bribe money his father had offered her all those years ago. She refused to provide ammunition in the battle between Nate and his dad, not when she worried Nate would be the one to come out wounded.

"And the other part?" Nate asked.

"The other part is angry. At the situation. At you."

Nate took a deep breath, quickly releasing it on a rush of air. "I deserve it. I know." He stepped closer. "But I have one question for you."

The intense gleam in his eyes had Sofía sitting up on the stool, wary about his intent.

"All these years, you're the one who reminded us of that 'no-strings-attached' credo. If my ill-fated, idiotic decision hurt you, could that by any chance imply you didn't like living by the rule? Could you consider giving it up?"

Ay, how she longed to believe a future with them was possible. But with Monday's meeting looming, and his father's influence a steady deterrent, anything more than what they had right now didn't seem possible.

"Sof? Could you?" He stepped closer, ducking down to peer at her.

He grasped her knees, the warmth of his palms on her bare skin beckoning her to lean toward him, fall into the arms she had once been certain would always catch her.

Now she wasn't sure if she could count on that.

"There was a time, when I thought…hoped that maybe…" She shook her head, terrified of baring her soul and opening herself up to potential disillusion and heartache again.

Regret swelled in her chest, pushing the tears clogging her throat to the surface.

"I can't do this." Not wanting to cry in front of him, Sofía hopped off the stool.

She crossed to the window along the left wall, stopping to stare at the darkened backyard. Through the blur of tears, she caught the vague outline of the banyan tree. It greeted her, a reminder of the importance of putting down roots and holding fast to what she valued.

For her, that was *familia*, faith, and love.

Mami and Tía Mili referred to them as the trifecta carefully interwoven to create a good life. There'd been a time when Sofía would have attributed some part of all three to Nate.

Since that first summer, when he'd fit in so easily at Tía Mili's, he'd become part of her *familia*.

Over time, she'd built up faith in him, in their ability to figure out a way to eventually be together.

And love. Her love for him would never go away. Being with him again now had opened her eyes to that indelible truth.

In the window's reflection, she watched Nate move closer, longing for the security of his embrace.

"I don't want to push you into anything you don't want. Or you're not ready for, Sof." His softly spoken heartfelt words pierced her soul. "I owed it to you, to myself, to be honest with you. I messed up. If I could go back in time and change things, I would. You asked for this week. These days together here, and I want to give you that. If you'll let me."

His hands hovered in the air near her shoulders. As if he was uncertain whether she would welcome his touch. He was a good man, her Nate.

Ooh, how she longed for him to be hers.

A tear slid from one of her eyes, leaving a wet trail down her check. Sofía spun to face him.

His expression fell when he caught the moisture in her eyes.

"Oh Sof, I don't wanna hurt you. I lo—"

He broke off as she threw herself at him, cupping his face with her hands to pull him down for her kiss.

"Enough talking," she murmured in between kisses. "Take me to bed, Nate. Please."

In a quick move that had her yelping in surprise, Nate crooked one arm under her knees to lift her into the air. He grinned down at her, a wolfish smirk that curled her toes with its promise of sin and seduction.

"I thought you'd never ask."

Chapter Eleven

"WHY THE *HELL* won't you freaking accept what I'm trying to do for you?" Sal bellowed.

Nate silently counted down, confident he knew what was coming in 3...2...1...

"Calm down," Sofía ordered. "Your doctor said to take it easy. Yelling at me and getting upset over all of this isn't good for you."

"Pshaw!" Sal complained. He slouched back in the outdoor wicker lounger Sofía had dragged over from the wooden deck, setting it under the shade of the sprawling banyan tree in Bernardino's back yard. The older man rubbed his round, well-fed belly like it might bring him luck and somehow grant his wish for a steak and potato dinner. "I'm already drinking this foul-tasting shake. It's enough of the doctor's orders for me."

Sal glared at the purplish concoction filling the glass Vivi had shoved into his hand before leaving to pick up a list of medicines at the pharmacy.

From his chair across the black wrought-iron rectangular table between them, Nate tipped his water glass in salute. If he had asked for a hearty meal and been handed a veggie protein shake instead, he wouldn't be too happy either.

"Back me up here, Nate," Sal cried. "Tell this ungrateful woman she should take the money I'm offering and guarantee herself that those small-town commissioners can't turn her bid down."

"You're forgetting he's the opposition here, Sal. Nice try, though." Sofía's blunt response was softened by the grin she flashed Nate from the wicker chair next to his. She brushed her fingers over his forearm in a light touch that drew his answering smile.

Still, the word "opposition" was like the prick of a sea urchin's sting, its spine puncturing deep into his psyche.

Joke or not, he feared that on some level, Sofía still saw him as the competition. That she couldn't separate him from Hamilton, Inc., and his father. If that couldn't happen, then the future he wanted for them was over before it even started.

"A little healthy competition is good in a relationship," Sal said. "Keeps things feisty, especially in the bedroom."

"*Ay Dios mío*, I am not having this conversation with you." Sofía mock-glared at Sal's hearty laugh. "Even my papi didn't give me 'the talk.' That was Mami and Tía Mili's department."

She rolled her eyes like the adolescent she had probably been when her mom and aunt had sat her down. Lips pursed in a good imitation of a pouty teen, Sofía finger-combed her curtain of dark hair, brushing it off her shoulder. A few of the silky strands clung to her bare skin and Nate gently brushed them aside, reveling in the opportunity to touch her.

Part of the poker chip tattoo on the back of her right shoulder peeked out from the edge of her halter-top blouse. His body thrummed, recalling the trail of kisses he'd placed along the outline of the red and green chips early this morning. Blood pooled low in his body as he remembered her moan of pleasure when he continued that trail lower.

Given their present company, Nate halted the memory replaying in his head and took a long pull of his ice water. This was neither the time nor place for him to relive their incredible nights together. Sal had been here over an hour, and the man was finally starting to warm up to him. No need to give Sofía's mentor any reason to doubt that Nate's intentions where she was concerned were anything less than honorable.

Earning Sal and Vivi's blessing was a key step along the path to being back in Sofía's life. For good this time.

Overhead, the sun had already started its descent behind the roofs and treetops. Thin clouds reminiscent of cotton balls that had been stretched thin spread across the blue sky. Paul's relaxing classical music channel played inside the house, the soft strains floating through the open windows.

While Sofía and Sal continued their banter, Nate relaxed in his chair, enjoying the nuances of their relationship. The older man was determined to front her all the money for the Paradise Key Resort bid. Her pride made her adamantly against any plan that didn't have her as the largest investor, something the bank had vetoed. Sal pushed, cajoled, and argued, but never crossed the line into ordering or belittling. He respected her.

It was a refreshing revelation—that people had mentors who believed in them.

Sal might not have an MBA from an Ivy League institution or a vast conglomeration of resorts and hotels in his arsenal, but he was remarkably business and people savvy. He didn't operate with smoke and mirrors and double talk.

No, Sal believed in shoot from the hip, "tell-you-like-I-see-it" truth. His devotion to Vivi and his family, in which he included Sofía, was evident based on the information he'd shared earlier regarding his will. Despite Sofía's insistence she didn't want Sal thinking along the lines of someone having to read the legal document anytime soon.

The New Jersey retiree had been equally as adamant about revealing its contents, admitting that should something happen to him, Sofía would receive Bernardino's outright. His and Vivi's two sons would split the other properties, with his adoring wife receiving the rest.

The news had come as a surprise to Sofía. She blanched, her tan skin turning a chalky shade, and she'd quickly shut down further talk of death and wills.

"Like I said already, you're not going anywhere, old man. You hear me?" She waggled a finger at Sal.

To which he'd laughed, taken a sip of his protein shake,

and then cringed. "I'll tell youse guys right now, I'm not sticking around long if this is the only thing I get to eat!"

"Is he behaving out here?" Vivi's high-pitched voice called from the open back door. She strolled out in white capris and a billowy bright floral blouse, her blonde bob miraculously as poufy as it had been earlier today, despite the humidity. White paper bag in hand, she shook it at Sal. "We're all set. I got everything."

"We? I'm the one stuck looking like a pill popper with all that stuff they prescribed. Not you."

"Hush, it's gonna keep you here. With me. With us." Vivi waved an arm to encompass them all, and Nate found himself wishing he really was part of their group. And not just for a few days.

Vivi sank into a reclining lounger next to Sal's. The older man reached over to take his wife's hand, raising it to his lips for a kiss. She smiled at him, her lined face the picture of love, relief, and hope.

Deep inside Nate, a pang of yearning burned, searing and sharp.

Sofía sniffled, knuckling a swift wipe under one of her eyes. He rubbed the back of his fingers on her bare arm, her tanned skin smooth and soft. Head bowed, she surreptitiously swiped at her tears and angled her chin to look his way.

Love for the older couple shone in her golden hazel eyes, the gentle curve of her smiling lips. Sal and Vivi were another example of commitment and the sanctity of marriage for Sofía. Along with her mami and papi, and Tía Mili and her late husband. They had all taught her the value and importance of *familia*. It was what Sofía deserved.

And what Nate had never offered her. At first because they'd been young and carefree, focused on their degrees and careers. He'd also been intent on following his mother's request that he keep the peace in their family, trying, though failing, to earn his father's respect.

Lines had been crossed with the engagement fiasco. But ultimately, Nate blamed himself. Pride and fear had kept him from revealing the depth of desire for Sofía. Some warped idea that he should play it safe, wait for her to admit her feelings first. That way he could protect himself if his love wasn't reciprocated.

Hell, he'd spent his entire life with a ringside view of the lopsided match between his indulgent mom and his ego-driven father. Nate had witnessed the pain his mom tried to hide, loving someone who didn't, maybe couldn't, return the same depth of sentiment.

Going back to New York with Sofía's stoic reaction to his father's edict, followed shortly after by her curt text that he not contact her again, had been the lowest point of his life. Yet, he had respected her wishes and kept his distance. Hating it. Missing her more than he'd thought possible.

And then they'd run into each other in Paradise Key.

Once again, the resort had brought them together.

That she'd allowed him back into her inner circle, that

he was here, part of her Key West *familia* in a way he'd never been before, gave him hope.

Sitting here listening to Sal's insistence that Sofía let him help her and Sofía's insistence she be the larger partner in any deal as some kind of proof to herself had been like the flick of a match across sandpaper, lighting the fire of a new idea in Nate's brain.

Originally, he'd thought, if he could prove that the Sarasota property was a better investment for Hamilton, Inc. they'd back away from Paradise Key Resort. Leaving it for Sofía to win.

But without solid financial backing, if her pride would not allow her to agree to Sal's proposition, her bid didn't stand a chance. Even if Vida and a couple others on the Local Planning Agency wanted to vote in her favor, in good conscience they'd have to pass. Sofía would lose.

The LPA might, however, look positively on another bid. If he could get Sal alone before morning, when Nate took his flight to Sarasota, maybe—and it was a big maybe, because Sofía's mentor would have to trust that Nate was on the up and up—he could turn this situation into a win for everyone with their fingers in the Paradise Key Resort pie.

"Oh, I almost forgot, Paul needed to talk with you about something, Sofía," Vivi said. She sat up in the lounger. "Here, I'll go along. He said it has to do with one of the other guesthouses, Vivi's Place, I think."

The two women crossed the wooden deck area, then disappeared inside.

Nate sat forward in his wicker chair. His window of opportunity had been opened.

"Sal, I have a proposition for your consideration. One that could ensure something important we both want—Sofía's happiness."

Sal cracked open one eye. He stared at Nate in the waning sunlight. His round face serious, considering.

Nate had played this game before across countless boardroom tables. Never had the outcome weighed as heavily on him as it did now.

The older man sat up. He leaned over to set the melting purple protein shake on the wrought-iron table with a thunk. "Okay, show me your cards."

"SOF. SOFÍA."

Nate whispered her name in her dream. His hand smoothed her hair from her face and she nuzzled into his warmth, seeking more of his touch.

"Sofía, I gotta go soon."

Go? The word finally penetrated her sleep to register, and she bolted upright in bed.

"What time is it?" She squinted at her cell on the nightstand.

"Almost six."

Nate perched on the edge of the mattress, already show-ered and dressed in navy chinos and a short-sleeved, sky-blue button down. With his duffle and hanging bag by the door, he looked packed and, *ay Dios mío*, ready to go.

Her heart dipped down to her stomach, then shot up to her throat.

"You sure you grabbed everything?" she asked, rubbing the sleep from her eyes.

"I'm all set. Just have to return the rental, then head to the airport. I didn't want to wake you, but I didn't want to leave without saying good-bye, either."

Like he had in her dreams, or maybe it hadn't been a dream after all, he tucked her hair behind her ear, traced the pad of his thumb along her jaw.

She grabbed onto his biceps, anchoring herself. Sudden-ly, everything had sped up out of control. The end had arrived. Much faster than she anticipated.

Nate fit in so well here. Paul flirted outrageously with him while singing his praises about how great Nate was assisting with staff and guests. Vivi had been smitten from the moment she heard Nate had driven Sofía through the night. Even Sal had given his gruff approval, something he'd never done with the few men Sofía had dated in the past.

But these last few days weren't reality. Nate couldn't dodge his father's phone calls indefinitely. Sooner or later—

"Don't," Nate said, interrupting her downward thought spiral. He leaned closer to press a kiss on her forehead, and she caught a whiff of her floral shampoo mixed with his musky cologne. A blend of her and him that made her ache with longing.

"You're thinking too much. Rationalizing why-not's."

"Because there are a lot of them," she answered grimly.

"Not really."

"Please." She sucked her teeth and dropped her gaze to the cream duvet, brushed a nonexistent speck from the material. "I've always understood that being a Hamilton comes with certain responsibilities for you. And believe me, I get it. My family relies on me, too. Sure, in different ways and…" Her attempt at a laugh came out sounding more like a strangled cough. "In different social circles, but expectations are expectations. I'd never want you to do something that could hurt your relationship with your mom. With either of your parents."

"You are the smartest, strongest, most compassionate woman I know, Sof. You're also one of the most hardheaded."

"Hey!" She gave his chest a push, matching his teasing grin with one of her own.

His green eyes flashed with laughter, and she realized she'd risen to his bait. Her maudlin mood had smoothed over thanks to him.

He put his hand over hers, trapping it against his chest. She longed to smooth her palm along the tempting contours of his muscular body like she'd done last night. But he had a plane to catch, and she had a real life to get back to. A resort bid to finagle financing for.

As quick as it had flashed, Nate's teasing grin faded. He stared at her intently. His eyes bore into hers as if he searched for something deep inside her. "Do you trust me, Sof?"

Her breath hitched at his question.

Somehow, she felt certain that more than she knew about rode on her answer. Fear rose to strangle her.

And yet…when she thought back on the past few days together, all he'd done for her this week and throughout most of their history. There was only one way to truthfully answer him.

"Yes, I do."

Nate's shoulders relaxed on a rush of breath. "Good. That's really good."

"But it still doesn't—"

He silenced her debate with a kiss. Sofía fisted her hand in his shirt, pulling him closer. She devoured his mouth, his tongue, savoring his minty taste, desperate to make this memory last. As if he sensed her anguish and sought to soothe her, he cradled her face with his palms and gentled their kiss. He slowly stroked her tongue with his before easing back to drop tiny, feather-light kisses on her nose, her chin, and what he liked to call his favorite corner of her mouth near her beauty mark. When he reached her forehead, he pressed his lips to her skin for several heart-wrenching seconds. Then, he stood and slowly backed away from her bed.

"Don't give up on us. Don't give up on me." His words were strong and steady, but in the depths of his beautiful eyes, he pleaded with her.

"I can't—"

"Promise me."

Her chest aching, she stared at him, wanting to believe that maybe, somehow…

"I promise," she finally whispered.

"Okay," Nate murmured as he bent to grab his duffle strap and sling it over his shoulder. He unhooked his hanging bag from the doorknob, then straightened to face her. "I'll see you in Paradise Key on Monday."

She nodded, unable to say anything around the grapefruit-sized lump of tears jamming her throat.

"And Sof, if at any time you have doubts about me. About us. Remember this… I love you."

Before she could respond, he slipped through the door, closing it softly behind him.

Seconds later, the floodgates opened on her tears.

¿Ay por qué? Why did life have to be so unfair?

Nate finally gifted her with those three words she had always longed to hear—*I love you.*

Only, they came days before his father and Hamilton, Inc. planned to try and crush her dreams. Again.

Chapter Twelve

S OFÍA STARED AT her reflection in the bathroom mirror at Tía Mili's condo, listening to her *tía's* lecture as it drifted down the hall from the kitchen.

"*Recuerda que tener mucho orgullo es un pecado, Sofía.*"

Yes, she remembered that having too much pride was a sin. But she also knew that not enough pride would get her trampled in the business world.

"Are you ready?" Tía Mili called. "It is almost six o'clock and the meeting starts at six thirty, *verdad?*"

"*Sí*, give me two minutes."

Bending closer to the rectangular mirror mounted on the wall above the shell-shaped sink, Sofía double checked her lipstick, then dabbed the edge of her finger underneath her bottom lashes to wipe away a little smudge of mascara.

"This is it. You can do this," she assured herself.

"Yes, you can." Tía Mili appeared in the doorway, her encouraging smile accessorizing her dark floral-patterned dress. It was her favorite, she'd said, and it would bring Sofía luck during the LPA meeting at town hall tonight.

Sofía pressed her hand to her stomach, trying, but failing, to calm the battalion of army ants marching inside.

Hopefully to a celebratory parade and not to the demise of her career dream.

"You look beautiful." Propping her shoulder against the doorframe, Tía Mili beamed at her. "Professional and approachable. Exactly like how you envision the resort. Vida and the others won't be able to turn your idea away."

"*Bueno*, since the best I have is an 'it's under consideration' from the bank in Key West, I won't be surprised if the LPA says no."

"Then you do it Sal's way. Better to own part of the resort than none at all, *verdad?*"

Heaving an aggravated sigh over her inability to secure funding on her own, Sofía leaned her hip against the bathroom's worn Formica counter. "Yes, that's true. But I'm going to submit my original plan first, and keep the second one ready to hand them as back up if needed. Sal helped me pull it all together over the weekend."

"*¡Ay, que terca eres!*" Tía Mili said on a groan. She flicked the blue kitchen towel she held at Sofía, then spun away.

"I thought you said being hardheaded was a good trait!" Sofía called out, chuckling at her *tía's* grumble in response.

Less than ten minutes later Tía Mili pulled her Ford sedan into an open parking space near town hall on Second Street. It was a quiet Monday evening with only a few cars cruising the road. Further down the sidewalk, a group of teens licked their ice cream cones in front of Delightful Scoops. It reminded her of similar treats shared with the girls. Of home and community.

Sofía paused, soaking in the memories and the emotions they evoked, allowing them to infuse her with confidence and determination.

The town and the commission had done a fabulous revitalization job the past few years. Jenna had mentioned how local businesses had chipped in, banding together with the LPA to replace older roofs with clay tiles, repair damaged stucco, and paint their building facades with eye-catching tropical colors. All with the idea of attracting family-friendly tourists to their sleepy little beach town.

That was where Sofía's plans for the resort came into play. She hoped the LPA would appreciate her vision and recognize her potential and commitment to their community. If only she had a definite yes from the bank, she'd feel a hell of a lot more confident.

They neared the building when Sofía caught sight of Jenna and her boyfriend Zach, who had apparently patched things up after whatever had gone down last week when Sofía was in Key West. With Evie having returned to Philly, Sofía had met Jenna and Lauren for lunch at Deli 2389 earlier today. Jenna had shared all the details of what Zach had organized to win her back. The guy definitely knew how to break out a grand romantic gesture when needed. Good, because her dear friend deserved them.

Jenna greeted Sofía with a tight hug and a passionate, "You're going be great in there. And you look fabulous by the way."

Sofía fingered the tie at her waist. Like Tía Mili, she'd donned a favorite outfit for confidence. The short-sleeved wrap dress hit her at the knee, and its black material with tiny white squares made a professional yet feminine fashion statement. She had pulled her hair back in a sleek, low ponytail secured at her nape and her shoes...

She glanced down at her sensible black heels, remembering them in Nate's hands the afternoon they'd run into each other at the beach. When he'd surprised her by offering his business advice. That had been a week ago today. So much had happened between them since then. So much still left undecided.

"Is he here?" Jenna asked.

"Yeah, he texted me earlier. We're supposed to meet up inside." Sofía gestured toward the pastel peach stucco building that housed the town hall. "On the battle ground."

"Hush, do not think of it that way," Tía Mili admonished. "*Dios* has a plan for you, *nena*, and I am confident that the resort fits into it."

In unison, Sofía and Tía Mili made a sign of the cross, pressing a kiss to their fingertips at the end as if they held a rosary's crucifix in their hand.

"There you go. It's meant to be then. If there's one thing you should know, Zach," Jena said, bringing her boyfriend into their conversation. "It's if you're on Tía Mili's prayer list, odds are good the Big Man is listening."

"I'll keep that in mind," Zach answered, earning a smile of approval from Sofía's *tía*.

"I always felt your young man showed promise."

Jenna blushed at Tía Mili's teasing. Zach grinned and put his arm around Jenna's shoulder to hug her to him.

Sofía chuckled, knowing her friend wasn't usually comfortable with public displays of affection, happy to see Jenna leaning into his embrace. "Okay, as much as I'm enjoying the love fest here, I see Vida's old truck parked across the street. We should get inside and let the Hunger Games begin."

"Enough with the negative talk, *por favor!*" Tía Mili smacked Sofía on the arm with her clutch purse. "*¡Sé positiva!*"

"I am being positive. Positively sure Tyson Braddock intends to make this difficult for me."

"He's like that with a lot of us. You're in good company." Zach held the door open for the rest of them to enter ahead of him. "I say, give him hell!"

Inside the lobby, a mini palm tree replica greeted them. At the far end of the short tiled hall ahead, people mingled at the entrance to the main meeting room.

"Lauren texted me. She's already inside, saving us seats in your cheerleading section," Jenna said, leading the way down the hall. "Sounds like more people showed up than usually do for a mid-month LPA meeting."

The nerves that had quieted in Sofía's belly flared to life

again, flitting about like a swarm of fireflies with electrical currents continuously zapping her system.

A door on the left side of the hall opened, and Nate exited the men's restroom. In camel chinos, a soft blue shirt under a navy single-breasted blazer, and having exchanged his usual Sperrys for a pair of cognac leather Oxford brogues, Nate could have easily walked off the pages of a GQ ad. The leather folio tucked under his left arm added the perfect touch.

Who wouldn't want to rely on someone with the Hamilton business reputation and charm to help Paradise Key continue their revitalization plans by resurrecting their beloved resort? Any positive vibes inside Sofía instantly wavered.

Then Nate grinned, his green eyes lighting with pleasure.

"We will wait for you inside, *nena*," Tía Mili said as they approached him. "*Hola Nathan, buena suerte.*"

"*Gracias.*" Nate brushed Tía Mili's cheek with a kiss as he thanked her for her good-luck wishes.

Jenna briefly introduced the two men. After a quick hug so she could offer Sofía a whispered, "You're a rock star! He better be aware of that!" she took Sofía's tote bag from her, then followed Zach and Tía Mili into the meeting room.

"It's good to see you," Nate said as soon as they were alone.

"You too."

"I hear Sal's doing okay, still giving Vivi a hard time

about those protein shakes, huh?"

Sofía laughed, relieved that he asked about Sal rather than immediately getting down to business. Then again, he'd always known how to talk her off any ledge she may have wandered onto.

"Uh, yeah, I don't see him becoming a fan of those shakes any time soon." They shared a companionable smile before Nate's expression changed to a serious one.

"Listen, can we talk for a sec?" He touched her elbow and stepped toward the lobby area, away from the people milling about the meeting room door. "I wanted to present something to you, a Plan C if you will. But I didn't have everything squared away until a few minutes ago."

"What do you mean?" It was too late in the game to be pulling out a new playbook. Especially one she'd never seen before.

"I spoke with—"

The town hall's front door swung open, and in strode the last person Sofía wanted to see here. Her gut clenched. Every negative thought Tía Mili had warned her to stop thinking instantly clanged alarm bells in her head.

"Dad?" Nate said, his wide-eyed, scandalized expression letting her know he hadn't expected his father to come strolling in either. "What the hell are you doing here?"

"I'LL REPEAT MY question, what the hell are you doing here?" Nate barked as soon as he'd shoved his father and gently nudged Sofía into an empty office located right off the town hall lobby.

Based on the black-and-white industrial plastic name-plate on the scarred wooden desk along with the framed photo of a dark-haired man and a preteen girl, he'd picked the mayor's office to invade. The man was already in the meeting room, so their privacy was probably secure. Nate dropped his folio on the desk top, then fisted his hands on his waist as he confronted his father.

Sofía had yet to say anything. She remained near the door, the pinched look on her beautiful face telling him she wasn't happy about being here.

"Hamilton business is taking place at this meeting." His father's haughty demeanor was in fine form as he tugged methodically at the cuffs of his long sleeves with two fingers, then tilted his head back to peer down his nose at Nate.

"No, that's incorrect. We discussed this yesterday. *After* I sent you my report with the recommendation we drop this property and aggressively make a play for the one in Sarasota."

Nate heard Sofía's murmured "What?" but he maintained eye contact with his dad. Determined to force his point. "The figures prove it's a much better business move for the company."

His father dug his hands in the pockets of his black trousers, the picture of bored nonchalance. Behind him, on the far wall that faced the window overlooking 2ⁿᵈ Street, hung a framed aerial photograph of Paradise Key. If Nathan Hamilton, II, was asked to name just one local landmark or favorite spot, more than likely he'd draw a blank. Nate could come up with a few. Sofía, she knew them all, or at the very least, she knew the people who'd gladly show them to her.

This place was her second home. To Nate's father, it merely represented a potential financial gain.

"Hamilton, Inc. will not be placing a bid on any property here in Paradise Key," Nate ground out, reiterating the words he had already told his father.

Out of the corner of his eye, Nate caught Sofía's start of surprise, as if she hadn't believed his previous statement. Damn it, he had wanted to share the news with her privately. Not like this.

"I heard what you said yesterday," his dad replied. "However, after speaking with Tyson Braddock myself, and learning who was leading the second bid for the Paradise Key Resort, well…"

The condescending glance his father shot Sofía had Nate's irritation boiling.

"Let's simply say I thought it wise that I head down. Ensure for myself that Hamilton, Inc.'s best interests were truly being pursued."

Sofía's scoff at his father's prickish words had the corner of Nate's mouth twitching with a smirk. Unlike many who quavered when confronted with Nathan Hamilton, II's imperious ego, Sofía glared back at him, arms defiantly crossed in front of her.

"Sorry to negate your *unwarranted* disappointment, Dad, but contrary to your belief, I am fully capable of doing my job. Quite well, by the way."

"Yes, Nathan, I am aware of that. I am also aware of your…personal connection here."

Again with the condescension aimed at Sofía.

She jutted her chin in a "*kiss-my-ass*" response.

Witnessing her silent battle with his father caused a strange sensation tingling the back of Nate's neck. Like a poison ivy itch warning him that he'd rubbed up against something unawares.

"I'm thinking two properties instead of one might be more beneficial for the company," his father announced, completely dismissing Nate's in-depth report. "If a certain party opted not to bid here, we could take both."

"This certain party isn't backing down." Sofía's voice was iron clad. Her expression stone-cold serious in a way Nate had never seen before.

He stepped toward her, seeking to reassure her that he in no way agreed with the idea of her giving up. She deserved the resort. But his father's next words to Sofía hit Nate like a sucker punch from out of nowhere.

"I understand that in your youth, you had yet to see the value of listening to my advice and accepting my generous offer. Perhaps with maturity, you can view this one different-ly."

Sofía's arms dropped to her sides on a shocked gasp. Her gaze flew to catch his, the mix of fear and regret in her hazel eyes confusing him.

"What are you talking about?" Nate asked his father, quickly turning back to Sofía because he knew she'd give him a straight answer. "What's he talking about, Sof?"

Several slow heartbeats passed. Indecision creased her beautiful face, tightening his gut with apprehension.

"Nate, I am so sorry," she finally said, sorrow etching her raspy whisper. "I didn't want to tell you."

"Tell me what?" He reached out to her, but Sofía stumbled back with a quick shake of her head.

She pressed a hand to her chest, pain radiating from her like a palpable force. "This isn't something I felt was my place to share. Not if it might cause a problem between you and your dad. Even if what he asked back then, what he's suggesting now, is reprehensible to me."

On her last words, she straightened her shoulders. Pivoting on her heel, she leveled his father with a damn good impersonation of his own patronizing glare. "You underestimate me, Mr. Hamilton. Worse, you underestimate your own son. Nate's a savvy businessman. And an even better person. You would benefit by taking the time to get to know him. And that—" She stabbed a pointer finger at Nate's dad, magnificent in her outrage as she stood up for him. "That's advice *you* can take to the bank."

His father's nostrils flared on a deep inhale.

Nate stood rooted in his spot like one of those Key West banyan trees buffeted by hurricane gale winds, struggling to stay upright.

Sofía clasped his hands with hers. Her calm voice and the candor shining in her eyes quieted the uproar of anger and confusion whooshing in his ears.

"I believe in you, Nate. And I believe in myself. So I'm going into the meeting now and what happens, will happen. We'll figure it out. I'll let them know you'll be coming in shortly, okay?"

He nodded, slowly coming to grips with this new revelation. Admiring her even more so because of it.

She gave his hands a quick squeeze, then left the office without another word to his father.

"Nathan—"

"No!" Nate sliced a hand through the air to silence his dad. "It's time for you to listen to me. *Really* listen."

Anger consumed him. He tamped it down, barely, scowling with outrage at his father. A man Nate thought he had seen stoop as low as he possibly could, until now.

"What exactly did you 'offer' Sofía before. Tell me the truth!"

His father closed his mouth on whatever half-baked response he'd been about to toss out, slowly nodding at Nate's demand. "Fine. I simply let it be known that she could have all of her college expenses covered in exchange for leaving you alone. No longer distracting you from the family path."

Nate reared back as if his dad had slapped him.

"For God's sake, you brought up the idea of transferring to a state school here in Florida." His dad jabbed an arm at the window and the lazy traffic idling by outside. "I couldn't have you throwing away a Harvard education because of some summer fling."

What was he talking about? Nate pressed a hand to his forehead in disbelief as he began pacing the ten-foot office. He combed through his memories in search of whatever the hell conversation his father referred to.

The old man painted the picture for him. "You came home after spring break your freshman year. You and your mother were chatting in the library, and you mentioned some fool-hardy plan to transfer."

His father's replay had to be of a conversation he'd overheard. The only time Nate remembered ever discussing his collegiate life with his dad, it had dealt with Nate's grades or his business classes. His father hadn't cared about much else.

All of a sudden, a stark realization hit him. Nate jerked to a stop in front of the window with its cheap metal blinds and pale green curtains. It didn't matter what his father had heard or misheard. That wasn't the issue here. The issue was that...

"You had no right to disrespect Sofía like that back then," he growled.

He whirled around to pin his father with a glare. "You have no right to do it here, today. Her manners might keep her from shaming her *elders*," he sneered the word, "or from putting you in your place, but…damn, I've been a complete idiot!"

He shoved a hand through his hair in frustration. "I've spent my whole life trying to make you and the Hamilton name proud. But today, knowing the appalling way you've treated the woman I love, proves how much time I've wasted. And you know what? I'm done."

Shouldering past his father, Nate snatched his leather folio off the desk, then stormed to the office door.

"Nathan, wait!"

He ignored his father.

"Son!"

The rare desperation in his dad's voice was the only reason Nate stopped. Hand on the tarnished doorknob, he kept his back toward his father, choking on his own disillusion.

"I'm going in there now to tell the Local Planning Agency that Hamilton, Inc. will not be bidding on Paradise Key Resort. I will also be sharing the news that I'm putting my financial backing—mine, from investments I've made on my own, apart from Hamilton, Inc.—behind Sofía's bid. If I'm lucky enough, she'll agree to let me partner with her to co-own the resort."

God, he hoped she would agree.

"You should leave now and head down to Sarasota.

Check out the property for yourself. I'll help with that bid if needed," he continued, "and then I'm done. If you've ever had any respect or an ounce of love for me, you'll let this stand. Do nothing to impede us. And never..." He angled his body to look his father in the eye. "Never disrespect Sofía again."

His dad swallowed, exhibiting the first and only sign of discomfort Nate ever remembered seeing. At the older man's curt nod, Nate left the office.

Palms sweaty, heart racing, he strode down the hall toward Sofía. Toward what he prayed was his future.

Chapter Thirteen

"DID THE LOAN officer in Key West provide a timeframe for the bank's decision? Or is the LPA supposed to refrain from accepting new bids indefinitely, until you have exhausted every avenue?" Tyson Braddock leaned forward in his seat like a hungry gator sunning itself on the banks of a Florida river, eagerly eyeing its prey.

Sofía refused to be intimidated. Standing in front of her second-row aisle seat, with Tía Mili, Jenna, Zach, and Lauren next to her, she gained strength from their reassuring nods. Zach's muttered "jerk" earlier when the commissioner had grilled her about a few fine points in her proposal had even brought a smile to her lips. Despite the nerve-wracking interrogation.

"I'm simply asking for the LPA to recognize the merit and value to our town found within the pages of my proposal," Sofía replied. Hands clasped at her waist to hide their nervous trembling, she trailed her gaze from one end of the head table to the other.

"Of the two bids, her plan for a family-friendly destination vacation resort more aligns with what Mayor James and the rest of the commissioners have been working on," Vida interjected.

Tía Mili murmured *"¡Sí!"* under breath at her friend's supportive comment.

Behind her, Sofía heard similar rumblings of approval from the crowd. Many of the downtown business owners had either closed shop or left their employees in charge so they could participate in a discussion and decision that would impact their shops and restaurants.

Miriam Deresiewicz from Deli 2983 had confided in Sofía at lunch today that she was in her corner. Mr. Bonner at Delightful Scoops had stepped outside of his shop to offer his support when she passed by on her way home. And Ivy, the fun-loving beautician and fellow Puerto Rican who was close with Jenna, had made it no secret she was rooting for Sofía. Having so many local business owners in her corner proved to be reassuring. Unfortunately, they didn't get a vote.

"Yes, I agree that Ms. Vargas's vision is appropriate," Tyson said into the microphone he had placed directly in front of himself on the long table, though the meeting room was small enough that a mic wasn't necessary. His booming voice carried through the speakers, quieting the rustling crowd. "But can we, in good conscience and in keeping with our fiduciary duty, vote for her proposal when we have a perfectly viable second option on the table?"

"Do we?" Vida countered. "I don't see anyone associated with that bid in the room. And unless I'm mistaken, their presence is listed as a requirement, correct?"

Once again, chattering started up amongst the crowd.

Tía Mili tugged on Sofía's dress skirt. "*¿Donde está Nate?*"

Sofía shrugged a shoulder, wondering where Nate was herself. The meeting had started twenty minutes ago.

Based on their "*what's-up?*" frowns, Jenna and Lauren had the same question. She shook her head and made a wide-eyed "*beats-me*" face.

Was he still talking with his father in the mayor's office? *Ay Dios*, if so, that did not bode well.

Walking away in the wake of him finding out about his father's machinations hadn't been easy. Part of her wanted to stay and defend him or stand beside him when he confronted his pompous dad.

But the meeting had been scheduled to start, and whatever happened between father and son needed to happen without her influence.

As it stood now, his dad's attempt to bribe her, again, didn't stand to matter. If Tyson Braddock got his way, Sofía's bid would be voted down whether they had a second option or not. Having Nate own the resort was better than some stranger.

"If you could wait!" Sofía raised a hand to gain the committee members' attention. "I'm sure Nate will be right in to talk about his bid. Once he's answered your questions, if it's allowed, there's another proposal I'd like to present."

Sal's. The one that made him eighty-percent owner because he'd be putting in the bulk of the financing. If it was her only shot, she'd take it.

Fred Pearson, a retired high school social studies teacher and the oldest member of the committee, squinted at his watch. "If the young man can't be punctual, is he really someone in whom we want to place our trust to revitalize our landmark resort?"

"Yes!" Sofía answered, "He is. You should—"

"That's a wise and frugal outlook, Mr. Pearson," Nate called from the doorway.

All heads turned in his direction.

Relief relaxed muscles Sofía hadn't even realized she'd been clenching in her stressful state. Then she noticed Nate's flushed face, as if he'd raced to the meeting. Or spent the last twenty plus minutes arguing with his father. About her.

Dios mío, what must he think about her keeping the secret from him? Would he be mad? Disappointed?

The thoughts sluiced through her, ramping up her anxiety.

Grabbing onto the bottom edge of his blazer, Nate gave it a brisk pull as he strode into the room. "My apologies for the delay. A bit of revelatory business popped up unexpectedly."

Reaching the front, Nate paused to shake hands with each of the committee members, cracking a joke with Vida before turning to gesture at the group of attendees filling the chairs. "Thank you for your patience. I don't want to keep everyone too late, so I'll get right to the point. Hamilton, Inc. will no longer be moving forward with its bid."

Gasps and exclamations of "what the heck" tittered from the crowd.

Regrettably for Tyson Braddock, his slightly profane response was heard by everyone thanks to the microphone. Chortles of laughter filtered around the room as Tyson covered the mic with a hand.

"However," Nate continued. "There is another bid I'd like to submit for consideration. I believe the Local Planning Agency will find this one difficult to turn down."

Sofía was a little surprised that Nate would introduce the plan she and Sal had drafted, but she reached for her tote bag under her plastic stack chair to withdraw her folder. Printed copies in hand, she stood up, ready to pass them out to the committee members.

She stepped into the center aisle, drawing to a stop when Nate gave her a nearly imperceptible shake of his head. She frowned, confused by his intent.

"This new proposal is put forward by a team of three individuals, led by Ms. Vargas, to include myself and Salvatore Bernardino."

Sofía's knees buckled and she sank into her seat, nearly slipping off the edge because she hadn't moved completely back out of the aisle. Tía Mili grabbed onto her arm to keep her from landing in a heap on the floor.

"May I?" Nate asked Vida, indicating whether he could set his folio on the committee table.

"Sure," the older woman answered.

"*¿Qué es esto?*" Tía Mili whispered.

"I'm not sure what it is?" Sofía smoothed her hand nervously over her sleek ponytail.

At the front table, Nate removed four bound documents from his folder, handing one to each LPA member. "I submit these with an important caveat. Because I was unavoidably detained earlier, Ms. Vargas was unable to give her final approval. Thus, should she have any qualms or edits, let the record show that we reserve the right to withdraw and resubmit, should the committee still be accepting bids."

Still reeling from her shock over Nate's announcement, Sofía barely registered he had stepped closer to her and now held out a bound proposal for her to take.

Tyson Braddock, who appeared to have recovered from his gaffe and had the document opened on the table in front of him, spoke up. "As the chair of the LPA, we will note the submission of a new bid in tonight's minutes. At this time, we will withhold voting to allow members time to assess the proposal. Are we in agreement on that?"

He waited for each member to voice their yes or no before continuing. "Should we have any questions, will the two of you, and perhaps Mr. Bernardino, be available?"

Nate looked to Sofía for a response. The hopeful glint in his green eyes sparked a similar hope within her.

Rising to her feet, she moved to join Nate at the front of the room. "Yes, I can remain in town should you like to set up a meeting."

"Same for me. We'll be at your service," Nate added.

"Good," Braddock said. "If possible, we'd like to have a recommendation to the commissioners and the mayor by the next town meeting in two weeks."

"Frankly, if these two team up and Sofía allows the bid to stay as submitted, I'm confident we'll have a decision before then," Vida tacked on.

In the audience, Jenna and Lauren grinned at Sofía, both flashing her two thumbs-up. Tía Mili made a sign of the cross, then looked to the heavens as she murmured what was more than likely a prayer of thanks.

As excited as Sofía wanted to be, there were still loose ends threatening to unravel. That Sal and Nate had schemed behind her back, while she'd been racing to get her second proposal finalized, left her perplexed and uneasy. On one end, she was grateful that two of the most important men in her life had banded together to help her. On the other, disappointed they hadn't included her in the process or discussion.

Tyson adjourned the meeting, cueing many conversations to ensue, some of which were not utilizing Tía Mili's preferred inside voices. Before she knew it, Sofía was engulfed in a group hug when Jenna and Lauren practically tackled her. Tía Mili gave Nate a more sedate embrace, capped with a pat on his cheek. Then she elbowed the girls out of the way so she could reach Sofía.

"Do you see, *nena, Dios* has a plan. *Te lo dije.*" She gave a saucy wink, her chuckle rumbling in Sofía's ear as they hugged.

Of course her *tía* wouldn't miss a chance to say *I told you so*, though lovingly.

"Now, I think you have dinner plans, *no*?" Tía Mili said.

"Um, not really. Do we?" Sofía looked from Jenna and Lauren, not remembering any plans for the evening. She'd been too focused on her actual presentation.

The girls shook their heads, then stepped aside as Nate drew closer.

He placed his hand on the small of her back, her skin tingling at his touch. "I was hoping you might want to grab a bite together. Discuss a few…things with me?"

Sofía looked from him to Tía Mili, wondering when her *tía* had gotten involved with the subterfuge. Her *tía's* wide smile matched her head bobbing nods of encouragement, her unspoken "Go!" communicated clearly.

"Will you have dinner with me, please?" Nate asked, his raw sincerity like a hand reaching inside to squeeze her heart.

Trepidation, nervousness, and love converged in one tsunami wave that crashed over her.

"Yes," she said, giving him the only answer she could.

The one she had always wanted to give, only he had never asked her the right question.

"YOU HAVE TO keep your eyes closed, or I'll grab a tie from my suitcase and blindfold you," Nate told her.

"When did you get so kinky?" she teased.

"Ha, wouldn't you like to know?"

With her eyes closed, she couldn't see it, but she heard his grin.

He drew the rental car to a stop without them having driven very far. That told her they were somewhere within a five-to-seven-minute radius of the town hall.

Nate cut the ignition, and she heard the leather seat rub as he turned toward her. "I'm going to get out to make sure everything's ready. You have to promise me you won't peek."

"You're no fun!"

"What is it Tía Mili says…patience is a virtue. Now, do I have your word?"

"Ugh!" Sofía muttered on an adolescent-worthy groan. He didn't respond, but she felt his nearness. She reached out a hand to find him leaning into her passenger seat area.

"You don't know how badly I want to kiss you right now." His voice was a raspy whisper that set goose bumps a flutter down her arms. "But I know you have questions that deserve answers, and the same goes for me."

Eyes still closed, she grasped the lapel on his blazer. Part of her wanted to tell him to hell with the Q&A. Why not jump ahead to the *kiss and make up portion* of the evening?

But that would only delay a potential roadblock if they didn't clear the air.

Not one to put off bad news, she pulled his lapel to bring him closer. "Hurry up and get this show on the road already."

"Damn, feeling bossy, aren't you?"

She released her grip, sensed him moving away.

His laughter faded as she heard him open, then shut, the driver's side door.

Enclosed in the vehicle and following his orders not to peek, Sofía strained her ears in search of any clue as to where they were and what he planned.

A short while later, her passenger door opened.

"Thanks, Frankie," Nate was saying. "I appreciate your assistance."

"Any time, I can always use the extra video game money," a young boy answered.

Frankie. Frankie. She repeated the name in her head, trying to pair it with the voice to figure out this new person who'd been in on Nate's surprise.

Wait, Frankie from church?

Of course. If Tía Mili was involved with this, she'd probably helped Nate hire the kid to put together whatever needed doing while they were at the meeting.

"You ready?" Again, the proximity of Nate's voice let her know he loomed in her space.

He took her hands in his to help her step out of the car,

then grasped her elbow to guide her across a paved ground. The smell of salt water and fish greeted her.

"So we're near the beach," she guessed.

"Maybe," Nate hedged. About twenty steps later—because of course she'd been counting—and they stopped walking. "Okay, now you can look."

As soon as she opened her eyes, Sofía laughed out loud, recognizing where he'd brought her. The picnic area and pier at Tía Mili's house.

A white cloth covered the cement cinderblock table. A votive candle, flame flickering inside the glass, nestled in the center. On one corner sat a pizza box from Angelino's, the best pizza on the island since she was a young girl running around in pigtails. Two bottles rested in separate ice buckets. One she recognized as her favorite champagne. The other—she squinted at the label—the other was a bottle of sparkling grape juice. Like the kind they'd shared the night of their first…

Realization dawned, and she clapped a hand over her gasp of surprise.

Nate had re-created their first date. From the tablecloth he had snagged in the resort's dining room, to the pizza they had ordered, to the bottle of non-alcoholic bubbly he'd bought because they were underage.

Tears filled her eyes and she blinked quickly, trying to keep them at bay. One slipped out to trickle down her cheek.

"Hey, that's not the reaction I was hoping for." Nate

softly wiped the tear away with his thumb pad. "These are happy tears, right?"

Hand still pressed over her mouth because she didn't trust her voice, Sofía nodded.

"Good," he answered with a relieved smile. Then he drew her forward, leading her to sit on the cement bench.

The LPA meeting had lasted barely an hour, allowing them to arrive here with thirty minutes to spare before sunset. At this time of day, the inlet and mangroves spread out in front of the picnic area and small wooden fishing pier were bathed in a swirl of purple, orange, peach, and red. The two street lamps had already kicked on, and soon they'd be the only light available. As teens, the shadows had provided cover for heavy make-out sessions. Until Tía Mili called for her to come in.

Now, Nate sat on the opposite side of the rectangular table, facing her. His expression serious, he steepled his hands in front of him.

"You're probably wondering about the proposal Sal and I put together," he said. "A little pissed that we didn't clue you in."

"Smart guess."

"It was only because we didn't want to get your hopes up. We waited until he'd gotten the green light, but it took longer than we anticipated."

She tipped her head to acknowledge his reasoning.

"And me..." Nate eyed her speculatively. "I'm wondering why and how you never told me what my father did."

No accusation, only genuine interest and admiration laced his words.

Sofía rested her forearms on the white cloth, relieved to finally talk about something that had eaten away at her for years. "Like I said, what I think about your dad is one thing, and I purposefully chose not to be around him. If you recall, the few times you invited me to an event where he might be, I had an excuse why I couldn't go."

Nate's face crumbled in disappointment. "I hate that I never realized that."

"You weren't supposed to. Not from me, anyway. He's your *papi*."

"No." Nate waved off her words. "There's a big difference between my father and yours, Sof. No comparison at all. You should know I quit the company tonight."

"What? No! Nate, please don't do that." She lunged across the table to cover his hands with hers.

"It was time. I should have done it years ago. I'm not cutting ties with my family. You've taught me plenty of things, and one of them is the value of family. *Familia*."

She stayed where she was, elbows digging into the hard surface, unwilling to let go of him. Praying their connection helped him deal with the hurt his decision must have caused him.

"My dad and I have issues to work out. For instance, I made it crystal clear that he is never to say or do anything to cause you distress again. And while I doubt we'll ever see many issues eye to eye, I'm certain he'll never respect me as long as I'm working under his thumb. I've made a lot of mistakes trying to please him. Not anymore. It's a good idea for me to start something new, something of my own. Or even better, something of ours."

The honesty and the love she saw reflected in his eyes was a one-two kick-punch combination to her heart, demolishing the flimsy wall she'd erected over the past two years.

"I recognize how important it is for you to be an equal partner in the resort. My hope is that you can recognize how much it means for me to be a part of your life. Part of your *familia*. Sal took all your paperwork into his bank. They're willing to give you a loan for a third of what's needed for the resort."

"What?" The word escaped from her on a rush of disbelief, and she sagged back onto her seat.

Nate slid off his bench, quickly moving around to straddle the one on her side.

"I don't...I don't know what to say," she stammered.

"Say yes. We'll be three equal partners. And maybe down the road, you and I can slowly buy out Sal's portion, if we want, when we're ready. Until you and I are invested fifty-fifty."

"Are you sure?" Her mind grappled with the very real, absolutely amazing idea of her and Nate co-owning Paradise Key Resort. Running it together. The place where everything had started for them.

"I've never been more sure of anything in my life." Nate tucked a lock of hair that had escaped her ponytail behind her ear, sliding his hand down to cup her cheek. "I already shared how I feel about you, Sof. I love you. I have since that first time we sat here, eating Angelino's and sipping fake champagne. Only, I've been too scared to tell you. Afraid you couldn't love me as much as I love you and I'd wind up getting hurt, like my mom with my dad. But not telling you how I felt, how I *feel*, that hurts more."

"Oh, Nate," she murmured, shame over her own inability to share her emotions overwhelming her. Pride having kept her from doing so. "I'm the idiot."

Her eyes burned with tears, and she buried her face on his shoulder.

"Hey, what are you talking about?" He cupped her nape, his other arm coming around to hug her. "You're probably the smartest person I know. Though I'm betting Sal would wanna lay claim to that title. But you're definitely the most determined."

She laughed, amazed that even in midst of his declaration, he could make a joke to lighten her mood.

Straightening to sit tall facing him, Sofía grabbed a hold of Nate's waist. Doing so grounded her. He grounded her. Made her feel unstoppable. With him by her side, as her equal partner, they'd conquer any doubts that fear or pride tried to put in their way. Together.

"What I said to your dad earlier, about you?" She paused, waiting for him to recall their conversation. "I meant every word of it. You're amazing at what you do. More than that, you're one of the most caring, generous men I know." Her fingers curled around his belt loops, anchoring herself to him. "If we're talking about who was afraid to reveal their true feelings, afraid of getting hurt, add me to that list. I love you, Nate. So much it aches in my heart." She placed a hand on her chest, emotion welling when he rested his gently on top of hers.

"So yes," she continued. "I want to be your partner. In the resort, but more importantly, in life."

Nate's eyes fluttered closed on her last words, as if he was letting them sink in, afraid to believe her.

Sofía sat forward, bringing her lips a breath away from his. "I love you, Nathan Patrick Hamilton, III. I always have. I always will."

She pressed her lips to his in a whisper-soft kiss. It spoke of tender feelings and promise. Of deep devotion. Of love.

Nate dropped his forehead to rest against hers and they shared a quiet moment, humbled by their self-revelations.

A seagull's cry pierced the air. Off in the distance, a boat motored by.

"Speaking of the way you put my father in his place." Nate waggled his brows, his lips curving in a wicked grin. "You were pretty bad ass in there. It was actually kinda sexy."

He laughed when she swatted his arm.

"This calls for a celebration, you think?" He pulled the champagne from its ice bucket, then made short work of unwrapping the bottle and popping the cork. After filling two flutes, he handed one to her.

"To the resort." He raised his glass in a toast.

"To our partnership." Sofía clinked her flute against his.

"To our love."

She smiled, a sense of peace reaching deep into her soul. "To our love."

This toast they sealed with a kiss.

One that took her back to the first night she and Nate had walked the shore, hand in hand in front of Paradise Key Resort. Now their resort. A place where their *familia* would grow and flourish, safe in the shelter of their love.

Epilogue

"ARE YOU SURE you do not want another serving?"

Nate patted his belly, smiling his gratitude at Sofía's mami as she reached for his empty dinner plate.

"*No gracias*, I'm stuffed already." He pushed his chair back to stand. "But you and Tía Mili cooked, so I'll help with the dishes."

"Nonsense, *mi amor*. Tonight is a celebration for you and our Sofía. We are so proud of you two. The new owners of Paradise Key Resort. Sounds *maravilloso, no?*"

"Marvelous is the perfect word, Mami." Seated beside him, Sofía covered his hand with hers on top of the dining room table at Tía Mili's condo. Puckering her lips, she pressed against his side, angling for a quick peck. A request he easily granted.

Anything she asked, he would give her.

"*Ay*, so sweet," Tía Mili teased from the kitchen where she'd started putting away some of the leftovers.

The comfortable sense of belonging wrapped Nate in a soothing cloak. He leaned into Sofía, pleasure filling him at the absolute rightness in his world.

Her parents had driven up from Miami to share in the

special day. Mami and Tía Mili spent most the afternoon cooking while Papi had read the paper and taken care of any heavy lifting or last-minute runs to the grocery store.

All that had taken place while Nate and Sofía sat in an office in the town hall signing the official paperwork for the resort sale. Sal had sent his power of attorney, so it was just the two of them. Exactly as Nate envisioned it being someday soon.

Afterwards, they'd returned here to join the *familia* for the tastiest dinner Nate had eaten in ages. Puerto Rican pork roast, pigeon pea rice, and fried plantains, with fresh slices of avocado garnishing their plates. Sofía was right. If they kept eating like this, they'd both have to up their run miles.

Or find another fun way to work off some extra calories.

"Well, if you don't mind, I thought Sofía and I might take a walk to the resort before dessert?" Nate said to the room in general.

He caught Sofía's papi's gaze, a silent assent passing from the older man to him. The exchange calmed Nate's jittery nerves, assuring him that he was making the right move.

"Of course, go enjoy the sunset," Sofía's mom answered. "We will be here waiting for you when you return."

"*Gracias, Mami.* Tía, as always, it was delicious." Sofía hurried to press a kiss to the other two women's cheeks, rounding out the good-byes with a hug for her dad.

As was their tradition, her father clapped hands with Nate, tugging him in for a hug as well. It was a new sensation, this expression of mutual affection between all *familia* members. One he found himself enjoying.

Sofía waited for him near the front door, her hair loose, a dark curtain in contrast to her bright yellow sundress. "You ready?"

Her sweet smile, the happiness coloring her cheeks and lighting her hazel eyes filled his soul with joy.

He was more than ready.

"We won't be long," he called to her family. "Just a quick look around, maybe a short walk along the beach."

"Go, go." Her papi waved them off. "*Dios los bendiga.*"

God bless them. In Nate's opinion, he certainly felt like they had been blessed.

Even his own dad had joined in the well wishes today, sending Nate a cryptic text earlier.

Make sure you review all the terms. I'm proud of you.

After a final wave good-bye to her parents and *tía*, Nate and Sofía headed out, taking the stairs outside, hand in hand.

"NATE, WHAT'S THE rush? I thought you wanted to do a walk-through of the property?" Sofía scrambled to keep up with him as he practically dragged her through the resort's empty lobby area.

"I want us to catch the sunset before it's gone. We can

do a walk-through later."

They reached the glass doors leading to the pool area, and Nate fumbled with the lock. He frowned, cursing under his breath at the key.

Sofía put a hand on his back, hoping it might calm whatever had brought on his anxiety somewhere between the condo and here. "What's wrong?"

"Nothing. It's all good." He flashed her a grin, but before he glanced back at the padlock, she could have sworn she caught a hint of concern in his green eyes. Whatever it was, she'd have to dig it out of him.

"Finally." The lock slid open, and Nate pushed open the doors. "Come on. Let's hurry."

Outside, he led her past the drained pool and the area that had been the old Tiki Hut restaurant, making a beeline for the walkway leading to the beach area.

The sky ahead resembled a watercolor palette of blues, purples, and oranges smeared across nature's canvas until it met the glistening ocean. At the end of the walkway, they came to stop so they could slip off their shoes. Nate placed his Sperrys alongside her tan strappy sandals on the cement edge. She marveled at the sight of them side by side. His and hers.

Her heart fluttered at the silly thought. She and Nate were far from talk like that, but a girl could dream.

"Here. Yeah, this one. I think." Nate hurried over to a shady palm tree off to the right. Hands on his hips, he eyed the tree from top to bottom. He leaned to the side, peering at the resort behind them, before straightening to stare at the tree again.

"Are you sure nothing's wrong?" she asked, stymied by his strange behavior.

Nate shook his head, his face actually flushing as if he were embarrassed. "I'm fine. Probably a little crazy, so you should heed that as a warning."

He winked playfully, but his words still didn't make sense.

"Okay." The word rushed out of him on a heavy breath as he slapped his hands together. "I'm pretty sure this is it."

"What's it?" she asked, cocking her head in question.

"The tree. Our palm tree."

"*Our* palm tree?" she asked, more and more certain that at some point along their walk, this darling man she loved had lost a screw.

Nate laughed. "I was kidding before. I'm not going crazy, so you can stop looking so worried."

"And yet, you claim this as our palm tree." Sofía tried, yet she knew she didn't quite hide her doubt.

"I need you to go with me on this, since there is a method to my madness. It started with a floral sheet you brought from Tía Mili's. We laid it out right here." He spread his hands to indicate the sandy area at the base of the palm tree. "Dinner consisted of chicken fingers and fries, courtesy of the Tiki Hut when you finished your shift."

"Drinks were ice cold, fresh-squeezed lemonade from the Deli, because you knew it was my favorite," Sofía finished, setting the stage for their first Paradise Key sunset picnic together.

Nate smiled. For the first time since they'd stepped onto the resort property, his shoulders relaxed. Though she still caught a hint of nervousness in his expression.

"Exactly," he answered. "That night, I *knew*. I mean, we were so young I'm sure I brushed it aside. But the adult me, if I could go back and give the sixteen-year-old me one piece of advice, it would be, 'Trust your gut, kid, it's leading you the right way. She's a keeper.'"

Tears filled Sofía's eyes at his words.

"Good advice," she murmured.

"Yeah, it's one I plan to take, if you'll let me." Reaching into his pants pocket, Nate got down on one knee.

Sofía sucked in a sharp breath. She reached out to him, then anxiously pulled her hands back, balling them in fists at her chest, suddenly overcome with nerves herself. Afraid this wasn't real. Praying it was.

"Sofía, you are and always have been the love of my life. You've taught me what it means to have a best friend, a confidante, a lover, an everything. That's what you are to me."

He withdrew a small black felt box, opening it to reveal a glistening Tiffany & Co cushion-cut diamond engagement ring. It sparkled in the setting sunlight as if beckoning her to say yes to a question he had yet to ask.

"Oh Nate," she whispered, overcome with emotion.

Hands pressed together as if in prayer, Sofía brought them to her lips. *Dios mío*, this couldn't be happening. In her wildest dreams, she had imagined, but never...

"There was a time when we lived by a silly 'no-strings-attached' rule," Nate told her, his voice strong and sure. No sign of his earlier nerves. It was like they'd jumped from him to her, and now bounced around inside her chest making her heart race.

"I don't want that anymore. I want all the strings that you've wrapped around my heart tied in double and triple knots. So I'm asking you, Sofía Milagros Vargas, will you be my wife? My partner? My soulmate? Today and always."

Sofía sank onto her knees in front of him, a sob tearing from her chest. "Yes! Most definitely yes!"

Throwing her arms around his neck, she confirmed her response with a kiss meant to curl his toes and leave no doubt about her intentions. She heard the little box snap shut, then Nate enveloped her in his strong arms, deepening their kiss.

"I love you, Sofía," he murmured in between nips of her lips, her neck.

"I love you more," she answered.

His chuckle tickled her throat as he nuzzled her, before capturing her lips once more.

With the setting sun behind them on one side and their

beloved resort on the other, Sofía reveled in the sense of peace curling around her heart, cementing their love, and the promise of forever in their shared embrace.

The End

The Paradise Key Series

After the sudden death of one of their friends, four single women who spent their summers at a beachside resort with their families return. The place they loved when they were young is falling apart, as are the lives of the four women. They each have their own reasons for returning, and their own secrets to keep. But as they bond together to restore a bit of their past, they find love in the beachside town, and the happiness they have sought all their lives.

Book 1: *Summer Love: Take Two* by Shirley Jump

Book 2: *Love at the Beach Shop* by Kyra Jacobs

Book 3: *Resort to Love* by Priscilla Oliveras

Book 4: *Small Town Love* by Susan Meier

Available now at your favorite online retailer!

About the Author

Priscilla Oliveras writes contemporary romance with a Latinx flavor. Proud of her Puerto Rican-Mexican heritage, she strives to bring authenticity to her novels by sharing her Latinx culture with readers. Since earning an MFA in Writing Popular Fiction from Seton Hill University, she serves as English adjunct faculty at her local college and teaches an on-line course titled "Romance Writing" for ed2go. Priscilla is a sports fan, a beach lover, a half-marathon runner and a consummate traveler who often practices the art of napping in her backyard hammock. To follow along on her fun-filled and hectic life, visit her on the web at www.prisoliveras.com, on Facebook at facebook.com/prisoliveras or on Twitter via @prisoliveras.

Thank you for reading

Resort to Love

If you enjoyed this book, you can find more from all our great authors at TulePublishing.com, or from your favorite online retailer.

TULE
PUBLISHING